P9-DIB-849

TERROR
AT BOTTLE CREEK

BY WATT KEY

Alabama Moon
Dirt Road Home
Fourmile
Terror at Bottle Creek

TERROR
AT BOTTLE CREEK

WATT KEY

Farrar Straus Giroux
New York

Farrar Straus Giroux Books for Young Readers
175 Fifth Avenue, New York 10010

Copyright © 2016 by Watt Key
All rights reserved
Printed in the United States of America by R. R. Donnelley & Sons
Company, Harrisonburg, Virginia
Designed by Andrew Arnold
First edition, 2016
1 3 5 7 9 10 8 6 4 2

mackids.com

Library of Congress Cataloging-in-Publication Data

Names: Key, Watt.
Title: Terror at Bottle Creek / Watt Key.
Description: First edition. | New York : Farrar Straus Giroux, 2016. |
Summary: "Thirteen-year-old Cort's father is a local expert on hunting
and swamp lore in lower Alabama who has been teaching his son everything
he knows. But when a deadly Gulf Coast hurricane makes landfall, Cort
must unexpectedly put his all skills—and bravery—to the test"— Provided
by publisher.
Identifiers: LCCN 2015021386 | ISBN 9780374374303 (hardback) |
ISBN 9780374374310 (e-book)
Subjects: | CYAC: Hurricanes—Fiction. | Survival—Fiction. | Swamps—
Fiction. | Alabama—Fiction. | BISAC: JUVENILE FICTION / Action &
Adventure / General. | JUVENILE FICTION / Boys & Men. | JUVENILE
FICTION / Family / Parents. | JUVENILE FICTION / Family / Marriage &
Divorce.
Classification: LCC PZ7.K516 Te 2016 | DDC [Fic]—dc23
LC record available at http://lccn.loc.gov/2015021386

Our books may be purchased in bulk for promotional, educational, or business
use. Please contact your local bookseller or the Macmillan Corporate and
Premium Sales Department at (800) 221-7945 ext. 5442 or by e-mail at
MacmillanSpecialMarkets@macmillan.com.

FOR ALL OF MY NIECES AND NEPHEWS AND
THEIR MANY ADVENTURES TO COME—

Lizzie Anderton, Koestler Anderton, Maddie Key,
Fisher Key, Mary Frances Key, Reid Key, Maysie Key,
Olivia Myrick, Hayes Key, Phillip Key, Eli Myrick,
Garrett Key, and Ellie Key

The hurricane in the following pages is fictional, but based on several real hurricanes I experienced. For more about how this story came to be, see my note at the end of the book.

TERROR
AT BOTTLE CREEK

1

DAD SAID IT WAS TOO EARLY TO BE WORRIED about the hurricane. So far, all the storms predicted to hit us that season had veered east into Florida. Besides, we'd been through plenty of them before. It was just part of life on the Alabama coast.

I wasn't so sure. The storm I saw on our television was big, and it was taking a different approach than the others. And with a name like Igor, it sounded cruel and deadly.

I looked out the window of our houseboat. I'd have to think about the hurricane later. At the time I needed to worry about Dad's two clients waiting outside in their truck. He was supposed to have been back an hour ago to take them on an alligator hunt. They'd come all the way from Mississippi and they were getting anxious.

I keyed the handheld radio and tried him again.

"Dad?"

He didn't answer, but I didn't expect him to. I knew he was just up the road at Mom's rental house, and he didn't want me to know. Ever since she'd walked out on us six months before, he'd been going over there and trying to convince her to come back. I knew she didn't want to see him. Sometimes I think he just parked in her driveway and stared at the windows.

I walked out onto the deck and looked up the riverbank. The tall man named Jim got out of the driver's side and leaned against his pickup under the utility light. He twiddled a toothpick in his mouth and looked at his watch.

"You get him?" he asked.

"He'll be here," I said.

The man scraped the gravel with his boot and frowned.

My dog, Catfish, trotted up the ramp and leaned against my leg. I knelt and scratched him behind the ears. There was a strong smell of fish about him.

"What you been into out there, boy?" I said to him.

He wasn't much to look at. A dirty yellow mix of terrier and collie I'd found wandering the riverbank a few years before. Catfish thumped his tail against the deck and whined and trembled with excitement.

"We're going," I said to him. "Just hold on."

He thumped his tail again.

I heard the short, heavyset man named Hoss get out of the truck. His feet crunched across the gravel.

"Maybe we ought to call it off," he said.

"He'll be here," I said.

"Well, we got—"

We all heard Dad's pickup coming down the hill. He stopped behind the two men from Mississippi and got out while pulling a ball cap over his head. He hefted his jeans, which always seemed to be falling off him these days. He'd been thin and wiry his whole life, but ever since Mom left he looked like he didn't eat anything. She'd sucked the life out of him in more ways than one.

"Anybody ready to get a ten-footer?" he said.

"We *been* ready, Tom," Jim said.

Dad approached them and shook hands with each. They grinned reluctantly. Dad put on his carefree act, which used to come naturally to him.

"Sorry about that, fellows. I'll make it up to you. Gonna put you on old No-name tonight. Big rascal I been watchin' grow for fifteen years."

"Sounds good to me," Jim said.

Dad turned and crossed the ramp onto the houseboat and rolled his eyes at me like some people just didn't understand. Well, I understood. He was wasting his time and everybody else's carrying on about Mom like he did. And it was embarrassing. But how does a thirteen-year-old tell his dad he's being a fool?

"They almost went back to Mississippi," I said.

"They'd be sorry, too. You got everything ready?"

"Yes, sir."

"All right. Go help 'em with their gear, and let's head out."

2

DAD WAS THE BEST RIVER GUIDE IN THE COUNTY. He took his clients out by himself during the school week, but I helped him on weekends. Now the alligator-hunting season had him busier than ever. The work was tiresome, but it paid more than his usual hog hunts and fishing trips.

I gave life vests to our two clients and seated them in the front of our eighteen-foot flats boat. It was an aluminum-hull, center-console jon with a ninety-horsepower Yamaha two-stroke outboard. Dad said he didn't like four-strokes. Said they were too expensive and complicated to work on. If he couldn't fix a thing himself, he didn't want it.

Catfish scrambled into the boat and got into position on an old towel in the rear corner. Meanwhile, I cast off the stern and bow lines. Dad cranked the motor and waited until I climbed aboard. Then he put the boat in gear and idled out into the river.

"You fellows got everything you need up there?" he asked the men.

"We're good," Hoss said.

Our clients seemed in better spirits now that we were under way. They both cracked a beer and toasted each other. I returned to the rear of the boat, got the spotlight out of the dry box, and plugged it into the accessory port on the console.

"You got the emergency gas?" Dad asked me.

"It's up front," I said. "We really going all the way to Bottle Creek tonight?"

"I reckon. Get off this river. We won't have anybody messin' us up out there."

The alligator Dad called No-name lived in a slough on Bottle Creek. It was about as far into the middle of the swamp as one could get. If a person had heard of the place, it wasn't because of the fishing or hunting. Near this creek, shrouded beneath a tall canopy of cypress and water oaks, are the ruins of an ancient Indian civilization. Archaeologists refer to the place as the Bottle Creek Mound Site. There are no roads to it, no markings on maps, nothing to even signify the place except for a faint footpath of white sand.

Dad continued idling out into the river, letting the engine warm up. I triggered the spotlight and waved it across the water, then triggered it off again. We wouldn't need it for a while unless we heard another boat coming. We'd run dark, without any navigation lights, until we got deeper into the swamp. At night it was easier that way. It wasn't legal, but we could see better, using the dark wall of trees rising on either side of the bayous to guide us. Lights or not, there was always the risk of hitting a dead-head, a submerged log or piling. But Dad had run the swamp since he was a boy, and he'd memorized where all the hazards were.

"Nice night," Dad said to the men.

The water lay black and still, pressed beneath the thick greenhouse smell of the heavy air. It was unusually warm for late September, and the frogs and insects still cheeped and pulsed from the marsh. Across the river the swamp fell away for miles, calm and peaceful. I looked up and studied the sky. It was cloudless and specked with stars.

"What you think about that storm out there, Tom?" Hoss said.

"We're here, ain't we?" Dad said.

"They seem to keep throwin' 'em at us this year, don't they?"

"Long as they keep throwin' 'em into Florida, I don't mind," Dad said. "You boys ready to run?"

The men shifted and steadied themselves on the bench seat as Dad accelerated the boat onto a plane. I glanced down at my shoelaces, making sure they were untied.

We'd both ride standing up in order to see better. If we hit something and got thrown out, it was important to be able to kick off our shoes. A person can drown easy with shoes on.

The boat leveled out and we were soon racing across a black mirror of water with the wind whipping at our hair. I knew we might not be the only boat running dark until we got deeper into the backwater. Usually we had the swamp to ourselves that time of night, but with alligator season in, there was no telling. I trained my ears to listen for engine noise and kept my finger ready on the spotlight trigger in case I had to flash a warning signal.

We veered off the Tensaw River into a small bayou where the trees rose and hung over us on either side. Dad played the steering wheel, gently brushing it right and left, each of us drifting into our thoughts behind the steady noise of the engine.

There used to be nothing I looked forward to more than going out with him. But ever since Mom left, things had changed. Now, even though Dad was right beside me, it felt like I was alone. And everything he'd taught me about the swamp seemed useless. I just didn't see the point in it anymore.

"You all right?" he asked me.

I kept my eyes on the trees and nodded. He knew what

was bothering me, but he was poisoned with her. He couldn't get her out of his head, and I didn't understand it. She was sure out of *my* head. I never wanted to see her again if I could help it.

"Been a while since we've been to the mounds," he said.

"Yeah," I said.

We used to hunt and fish along Bottle Creek, but it had been a couple of years since we'd made the trip. The first time he showed me the mounds is one of my most vivid memories. He took me back there late one afternoon when I was six years old. We left the jon nosed into the brush, and he hefted me onto his shoulders and ducked into the narrow trail. After a few yards the trail widened under giant cypresses and water oaks. The swamp was suddenly dark and cool and strangely still. The only sounds were mysterious bird calls distant and shrill from the high canopy. Raspy green palmetto plants and large mossy vines made it feel like a lost land from the dinosaur age.

He carried me for nearly a half mile before I saw the mounds rising out of the gloom. They were eerie and ivy-covered and something from another realm, a long time ago. The first few hills were no higher than Dad's waist. As we continued they grew larger until we arrived at the highest, nearly fifty feet tall, rising into the canopy. He set me down and I followed him up the steep incline until we arrived at the top. We stood there beneath an old juniper, staring into the branches of the canopy beyond.

"Hit that left bank," Dad said, interrupting my thoughts.

I triggered the spotlight briefly on the riverbank ahead. Just enough for him to see a dark gap in the trees. He nodded and started a slow turn toward it. After thirty minutes of weaving through a maze of creeks and sloughs, he eased back on the throttle. The boat sat down in the narrow creek and we continued on, idling slowly beneath the Spanish moss and cypress limbs.

"All right, fellows," Dad said. "Let's get us a gator."

3

DAD KILLED THE MOTOR AND WE DRIFTED QUIETLY on the black water of Bottle Creek. I walked to the front of the boat, plugged in another spotlight, and gave it to Jim.

"Shine it up ahead of us," I told him. "Look for orange eyes glowing on top of the water."

Jim and Hoss both turned in their seats, and Jim began waving the light across the water and under the overhanging trees. I returned to the stern and sat in the jump seat beside Catfish and scratched him on the neck. Dad sat down in the chair behind the steering console and used the other spotlight to do his own searching.

"You boys heard of the Bottle Creek Indian mounds?" Dad said.

The men shook their heads, still studying the dark water.

"You get off in the woods to your right, and you'll run up on 'em. Like Inca ruins back there."

Jim turned and put his light on the trees, but there was

nothing to see except a dense tangle of palmetto and vines and Spanish moss.

"Way out here?" Jim said.

"About seven hundred years ago," Dad continued, "ancestors of the Creek and Choctaw Indians came down from middle Alabama to build a city in the swamp. There's eighteen mounds out there. They say there was thousands of Indians lived on top of 'em for hundreds of years. Then they all just disappeared."

"What happened?" Hoss asked.

Dad shrugged. "I bring archaeologists out here sometimes. From the University of South Alabama. They dig around and try to figure stuff out. Said maybe Hernando de Soto killed 'em. Maybe diseases. They don't know."

"I never heard of it," Jim said.

"Not many people have. It's too far in the middle of nowhere. No roads or nothin' to get to it."

"Who owns this land?" Jim said.

"U.S. government. There's an old metal sign back there sayin' it's a National Historic Landmark. Twenty years ago I brought the fellow out here that put it up . . . I figure that's the last time the government set foot in this place."

The men kept staring at the trees, probably thinking about the mounds. I'd thought about the mounds enough. And I already knew plenty about alligators and just about everything else in the swamp. Instead I wondered what my neighbor Liza Stovall was doing. Probably out with her friends somewhere. She was in my same class at school. We rode the bus together in the mornings along with her six-year-old sister, Francie. But Liza had a different life and different friends. Friends with real houses and places other than a giant dark swamp to go on weekends. It didn't bother me as much before Mom left. Now the thought of being left out was constantly on my mind.

"Better get your light on the water again," Dad said to the men. "Around this bend we'll come to a slough on the right. He ought to be there."

A light breeze brushed the tops of the swamp canopy. I looked up and saw the leaves trembling and thought about the hurricane again. Thought of it hundreds of miles away. Even if it didn't hit us, if it just came anywhere close, we'd be working for days getting not only ourselves ready but everybody else at the river landing.

As the current took us around the bend I saw the orange eyes reflecting in Dad's spotlight beam about twenty yards ahead. Catfish twitched and growled deep in his throat.

I put my hand on his head. "Easy, boy," I said to him.

Dad switched the light off and set it on the floor. He'd seen the gator, too, but he'd give his clients a chance to discover it for themselves.

Jim swung his beam over the creek, passing over the eyes once, then jerking the light back. "I see something, Tom," he said.

Dad stood up quietly. "Keep it on there," he said. "Yep, there he is, fellows."

"He's a big one," Hoss said.

"I told you," Dad said. "Cort, get the .22 out of the dry box and get it loaded. Hoss, grab that deep-sea fishing rod behind you and stand on the bow with it. Jim, you keep the light on him."

Hoss stepped onto the bow with the fishing rod. It was spooled with hundred-pound braided line and a weighted treble hook made for sharks.

"Those eyes are nearly a foot apart," Jim said.

Ten inches was more accurate, each inch representing about a foot of body length. But Dad wasn't going to spoil their excitement.

"Cast that hook over his back," Dad said. "Then reel it slow and snag him."

"We gonna reel him in?" Jim asked.

"No, but we'll wear him out," Dad said. "Then pull up to him."

It was a strange way to hunt, but the hunting regulations required that the alligator be harpooned or snagged and secured against the gunnels before you could shoot it.

"He can't get in the boat, can he?" Jim asked.

"He won't get in here, but don't stick your hand out after him."

Our two clients didn't know much about alligator hunting, but they'd been sportsmen all their lives and knew how to cast a fishing rod. Hoss arced the treble hook down the creek and made an almost perfect cast just over the gator's neck. Then he reeled slow until the line was taut.

"Hit it!" Dad said.

Hoss yanked the line, and the gator swirled the water and dove for the creek bottom. The fishing rod bowed and whined as the line spooled against the drag.

"Whoa, son!" Hoss yelled as he leaned into the strain.

"Keep the light on that line," Dad said. "We're just gettin' started."

4

HOSS STRAINED AND SWEATED AGAINST THE alligator. At one point I had to go to the front of the boat and pour water in his mouth and over his head. He leaned into the fight for thirty more minutes before the gator surfaced again. By then we were ten feet from the beast, ancient and black and smelling of fetid river mud. It only took a moment for him to see us and dive again. Then the bull towed us downstream for an hour while Hoss kept tension on the line and reeled when he could.

When the gator eventually tired, he stopped swimming and settled on the creek bottom like a boulder. Hoss reeled steadily, and the line began to angle down as we pulled the boat toward it.

"Give me the light, Jim," Dad said. "Cort, pass him that rifle."

"You think he's done?" Hoss grunted.

"He's about to be," Dad said.

Jim passed the spotlight to Dad, and I chambered a round into the .22, made sure the safety was on, and handed it to Jim. Hoss took one hand off the rod and wiped his forehead with his shirtsleeve.

"Now, listen up," Dad said. "Here's what we're gonna do. Hoss, you bow up on that rod and he'll come up next to the boat. When he does, Jim—I mean, as soon as you see him—you put a round right between his eyes. You got one shot. You hit him wrong, and he's gonna go nuts. Got it?"

Jim stared at the water and nodded.

"Go ahead, Hoss," Dad said. "Lean back on it."

Hoss got to his knees, leveraged the rod in his crotch, and started cranking. Dad held the light on the thin, dripping line disappearing into the murky creek. Slowly, the line began to quiver and rise.

"Safety's on," I said.

Jim clicked the safety off, brought the rifle to his shoulder, and pointed the barrel at the water.

The gator suddenly appeared out of the depths, rising like a black log beside us. Jim fired quickly, and the bull bucked and rolled.

"Hold it, Hoss!" Dad yelled.

The shot was a good one, and in a moment the gator hung limp next to us.

"All right," Dad said. "Good shot. Jim, you back off and let us get a line around him. Cort, get the rope."

I retrieved a coil of three-quarter nylon line out of the

dry box. I squeezed past Hoss, leaned over the gunnels, and started running it under the gator's neck. The moment my fingers brushed the scaly hide, No-name erupted. He bucked and twisted his head, and I smelled his rotten breath and saw a hundred yellow dripping teeth in my face. I was already falling backward when the tremendous jaws slammed shut inches from my shoulder.

"Hey, son!" Dad yelled. "What the hell you doin'?"

I lay on the cold aluminum deck, breathing hard, my mind racing and tangled with confusion.

Dad yanked the rope out of my hands. "You wanna get yourself killed?"

Hoss strained on the line, waiting for the gator to settle again. Dad stood over me, staring down at me like he wanted to make sure I was still alive.

Dad let out a deep sigh. "Lord," he said. "You know better than to dive in there like that."

I didn't have anything to say. I *did* know better. A reptile's reflexes last long after it's dead. You can't assume anything.

"He all right?" Jim asked.

Dad nodded and turned away from me. I could see he was shaken up as well. "Yeah, he's all right . . . Everybody, just hold what you got and take a minute."

I was embarrassed and I was ashamed. Now, more than ever, I didn't want to be out there killing stupid alligators with two men from Mississippi we barely knew. I just wanted to go home and go to bed.

After a moment I got off the deck and went to sit beside Catfish in the stern. I stroked my dog's back while Dad and the two men secured No-name.

It was midnight before they had the gator fully lashed to the side of the jon and we started the slow haul back to the boat landing. Jim and Hoss popped more beer and celebrated and seemed to forget all about my close call. Dad steered us slowly through the dark, cheeping swamp, his mind on something. Whether it was me or Mom, I couldn't tell.

5

TEN O'CLOCK THE NEXT MORNING I HEARD DAD GET up and make coffee. I lay on my back for a while, staring at the yellow water stains on the ceiling, thinking about the giant alligator mouth.

When I heard Dad step outside I climbed down off my bunk, pulled on my clothes, and went into the kitchen. I saw him through the window, standing on the back deck, looking over the river. I went to the counter and turned on our small portable television. I watched the storm on the news, looking like an enormous saw blade spinning over the Gulf. Landfall was predicted some time on Monday with the cone of probability centered on Biloxi, Mississippi. That was nearly a hundred miles southwest of us, but it was only Saturday and there was still plenty of time for it to change course.

I turned off the television and got a box of Raisin Bran out of the cupboard and poured it into a bowl. I was walking to the refrigerator for milk when Dad came through the door again. He went to the coffeemaker and poured another cup.

"Hurricane's headed for Mississippi right now," I said.

He took a sip of coffee and rubbed his eyes. "Yeah?" he said.

"You wanna see it?"

He studied me for a moment like more than one thing was going on in his head. "No," he said. "I guess it'll do whatever it's gonna do."

Dad leaned against the counter and took another sip. He was still thinking about something else. "You know you almost got your arm bit off last night?" he said.

I looked at the floor. "I know," I said.

"I mean, what was that all about?"

I shrugged.

"You got to always be thinkin' out in that swamp. It's a pretty place, but you pull back the curtain and it gets evil real quick. Understand?"

"Yes, sir."

He took another sip of his coffee and said, "Good."

"Figure we ought to start getting things ready?" I said.

He didn't answer me.

"Dad?"

"We got time," he said. "I need to run some errands."

"How long you gonna be gone?"

He got his cap off a nail on the wall and slipped it on. "I don't know," he said. "I'll be back after a while."

I finished my cereal and went outside and up into the dirt parking lot above the riverbank. Catfish swung in beside me and I knelt next to him. I rubbed his head as I ran my eyes over the landing. The property consisted of about five acres gently sloping down to the river. At the top of the hill was the Stovalls' three-bedroom brick house. Their family had owned the property since the Civil War. Some of the giant, moss-draped live oaks were even rumored to have been planted by their ancestors. Just downhill from the house was a storage shed, a bait shop, and a grass parking area. Part of the parking lot was used as a boatyard where customers left their boats on the trailer for free. Below that was a launching ramp and a steel money box where they could shove five dollars through a slot and put their boats in. Beside the ramp were two rows of covered stalls where some paid twenty-five dollars monthly to leave their boats in the water.

For seven years I'd lived in the same houseboat, moored at the same spot on the south end of the property. Five years ago Mr. Stovall had died of cancer, and ever since then Dad had maintained the grounds in return for free rent. The work mostly consisted of keeping the grass mowed, but we also made repairs when they were needed. When the river got high it sometimes tore out the catwalks. The north wind occasionally blew sheet tin off the roof of the boat stalls. Twice a year we hauled in gravel to fix the muddy spots in the road. Outside of these basic chores we helped people launch their boats and cleaned their fish and wild game. The place felt like it was ours, but all we really owned was the houseboat and the jon tied to the back of it.

Dad used to talk about building a real house when Mom was around. Mostly because he knew that's what she wanted to hear. Mrs. Stovall even offered to sell him a half acre up the hill, but Dad had enough problems just paying the bills he already had. There was not much money in being a river guide. With Mom it was always about the money, even though she was too lazy to work for it herself. She wanted Dad to change. She wanted him to leave the river and move into town and get a normal job that paid more. Even I knew that was impossible. The swamp ran in his blood all the way back to our Creek Indian ancestors. Taking the river away from him would be like taking the farm from a farmer.

I stood and crossed the parking lot to an old basketball goal Dad had put up for me a couple of years before. The net was torn and barely hanging on, and the pole was slightly bent from someone backing a boat trailer into it. I picked up a mud-splattered basketball and brushed it off. I took a step back and flipped it at the backboard. The ball passed cleanly through the hoop and landed with a dull, bounceless slap onto the dirt beneath.

"Thinking about playing again?" I heard Liza say.

I turned and saw her coming down the hill toward me. She always looked so fresh and clean and free of worries.

"No," I said.

She came up to me and fingered her blond hair behind her ears. We'd known each other since we were kids, but in the past year I'd started to feel different around her. I got nervous and uneasy. Sometimes I wanted to be with her all the time, but then I didn't want to be around her at all.

"Looks like you just need some air in the ball."

I frowned. "And somebody to pick me up after practice."

"I told you we can give you a ride on Tuesday and Thursday after band."

I looked at the ground and scraped the toe of my tennis shoe in the dirt. "Yeah, I know. But that doesn't solve the rest of the week."

"There's got to be a way, Cort. You were so good."

"I don't know. Maybe when this mess with Mom and Dad gets straightened out. We'll see."

"You gonna be around today?"

"I don't know where else I'd go. Right now I'm just waiting on Dad to get back so we can get ready for the hurricane."

"You think it's coming?"

"The news says it's probably going into Biloxi. That'll put us on the east side of it. Dad says that's the worst side to be on."

"Want some help?"

"I don't know what we're supposed to do yet. Dad's out running errands."

"Come up for lunch. Mom's cooking spaghetti."

"I just ate breakfast. We were out late last night."

Liza gave me this cute little smile she always made at the edge of her mouth. It was enough to make a person feel better about anything. "Well, come eat again," she said.

I smiled at her. "Yeah, all right. I'm gonna walk around and check on things. I'll be up in a bit."

6

I CROSSED THE YARD TO THE BAIT SHOP AND made sure the minnow tank pumps were running and the crickets had plenty of food. Then I looked out over the stalls and made sure none of the boats were hung up or listing. After everything appeared in order I made the short walk up to the Stovalls' house and knocked on their door. Francie answered, holding her Elmo doll that she carried everywhere.

"Hey, Francie."

"We saved some for you, Cort."

"Sounds good," I said.

I followed Francie into the kitchen, where Liza was at the sink wiping a pot clean. She turned to me and smiled. Mrs. Stovall was beside her, leaning over the counter making a grocery list. She was always calm and level-headed, nothing like my mother. Sometimes I wished Dad and Mrs. Stovall would get married and we could all just get together and be a normal family in a brick house.

"Help yourself, Cort," Mrs. Stovall said.

"Thanks," I said.

"Sit down," Liza said. "I'll get it for you."

I sat at the kitchen table. Liza heaped a plate with spaghetti and set it before me. I ate hungrily while she watched. Mrs. Stovall set a glass of milk before me and stepped back to lean against the counter.

"Think we'll be okay, Cort?" Mrs. Stovall asked.

I swallowed. "I don't think the river will get up here," I said. "But Dad might want us to board your windows."

"I think there's still a bunch of plywood behind the shed," Liza said.

I took a swig of milk. "Yeah. There should be enough."

Francie climbed into a chair next to me and put her chin on the table. "Where's Catfish?"

"He's out there waiting on you," I said.

"Does he stink today?"

"Probably. Maybe he needs a bath."

I looked at Mrs. Stovall and she rolled her eyes.

Francie got up and started for the door. "I bet he does," she said. "We should call him Stinky."

Liza and I laughed.

"Lord," Mrs. Stovall said. "Sounds like there's going to be two baths."

We heard Francie go out the door. I took another bite and turned to Liza. "What are you doing this afternoon?"

"Going over to Laura's. Nothing much."

She knew how I felt about being trapped at the landing all the time. Whatever she had planned, she didn't rub it in. I was sure she was going to be with all her friends from school. They were probably going to a movie that night or meeting up some other place fun. Doing what normal teenagers do.

"What's your mom gonna do?" Liza said, changing the subject.

I swallowed. "About what?"

"About the hurricane."

"I don't care what she does."

Mrs. Stovall frowned and turned back to the counter.

"I can't do anything about her," I said. "We got enough to do already."

"You and your dad are welcome to stay up here," Mrs. Stovall said.

I heard a vehicle and looked out to see Dad's truck passing the window. "Looks like he's back," I said. "I'll let him know."

"You can't stay on the houseboat," Liza said.

I shoveled the last of the spaghetti into my mouth and got up from the table.

"Well, I'm not staying at Mom's house," I said. "I better head down there and help Dad get ready."

Mrs. Stovall turned and took my plate from me.

"It was good," I said. "Thanks."

"Anytime," she said. "Come back for supper if you like."

I nodded to her and started out the door.

"See you later, Liza."

"Bye, Cort."

7

I FIRST MET LIZA WHEN WE WERE BOTH FIVE years old. Until then my family's houseboat had been tied at Live Oak Landing, a few miles downriver. Dad told me the property was sold and the new owner wanted the riverfront cleaned up and the houseboats gone. He knew Linda Stovall from grade school and had seen her family on the river all his life. He worked out a lease with Jerry Stovall, and we pulled the spuds and moved upriver.

Jerry Stovall had been about the same age as Dad. He was raised in the pine forests of north Alabama and inherited the landing when he married Linda. Dad described him as fair and reliable. Especially when compared to Dad with all his high energy, Mr. Stovall seemed nice but boring.

I remember Liza following him about the riverfront as he tended to the endless piddling and straightening required of the landing. She was always close to him, sitting on a five-gallon bucket or in the grass with her legs pulled under her, fingering her hair away from her face.

Mr. Stovall talked to her in his soft-spoken way while she nodded and smiled and laughed. When they walked up to the house together, he put his arm around her and pulled her close. Dad did the same with me, but somehow Mr. Stovall's words seemed to sink into a person a little deeper.

We didn't have other children our age nearby, so Liza and I were default playmates. I didn't mind that she was a girl. She was always interested in whatever I was into. And with Mom not wanting me around, I was usually into something outside. We explored the creeks and woods around the landing and helped Mr. Stovall with repairs to the rental equipment and bait shop. Sometimes we entertained ourselves with simple, quiet things like collecting tadpoles, arranging the pump house into a pretend general store, and poking at the giant black lubber grasshoppers that chewed lazily on the marsh grass. Mr. Stovall had learned plenty about running a river landing, but he hadn't been raised on the river like Dad. Liza was fascinated with what we knew about life in the swamp, and I was proud to show her the things Dad taught me.

Liza was tough. I admired the way she could see a thing for what it was and laugh about it. She didn't get silly and irritable like other girls I knew.

Things changed when her dad died. I never saw her

33

cry, not even then. But she got quieter. Her eyes lost the spark of curiosity. She was no longer interested in black grasshoppers and poking about the landing. If she came down to the riverfront, it was only to check on Francie or to pass along a message.

"I want to move away from here," she once told me.

The words hit me in the gut. Back then, I couldn't imagine wanting to live anywhere else. And I had never imagined not having her in my life.

"Why?"

"Because everything reminds me of him."

For a while I expected them to leave, and the thought of it sat inside me like a small sickness. I knew that even if they wanted to stay, it wasn't possible for Mrs. Stovall to run the landing and raise children at the same time.

"Linda oughta dump this place," Mom said. "Take the money and run."

"It's been in her family for years," Dad said. "She was raised here."

"Yeah, so what?" she said.

I think Mom hoped they'd sell. So maybe we'd have nowhere to moor the houseboat and have to move off the river.

Then Dad took to maintaining the grounds, and suddenly it seemed everything was going to work out. He even built a new row of boat slips to bring in extra rental income.

"She's gonna make more money off this place than she would workin' at Walmart," Dad added. "And she gets to stay home with her kids."

"Sure," Mom said, "while we do all the work."

I never saw Mom work at anything except making Dad miserable. But he knew it was useless to argue with her. He just nodded and stepped outside.

For now, it didn't seem like the Stovalls were going anywhere. But I often wondered if losing her father had ruined Liza for life on the river.

8

I FOUND DAD DOWN AT THE HOUSEBOAT LOADING A cooler into the jon.

"What you been doin'?" he asked me.

"Waiting on you."

"You got to wait on me for everything? We need to run that trotline and bring it in."

I could see he wasn't in a good mood. When Mom had been around he had always been happy, even when she wasn't. He was like a big kid, running from one thing to the next, excited about everything. Just the fact that she was there, that she was his, was all he needed. Now it seemed she'd torn his spirit out and gone up the road with it.

I cast us off and stepped into the jon as he cranked the motor. We ran upriver to where the long string of hooks was pulled tight across a sandbar. Imagine a clothesline with pieces of two-foot string tied all the way down it and spaced about six feet apart. On the end of each string is a fishhook, usually baited with pieces of mullet or eel.

Mullet is more plentiful, but eel meat is tougher and stays on the hooks longer. But catfish will really eat just about anything. We'd even caught them on chunks of Ivory soap before.

Dad eased the boat up to the bank, and I grabbed the end of the line where it was tied to a tree limb. The other end was anchored out in the river with a cinder block. I could tell we had at least one fish on by the way the line trembled in my hands. Dad shut off the engine and sat down while I pulled the boat toward the first hook.

"There's *something* on there," I said.

Dad didn't respond. It could be anything. We'd caught turtles, trout, flounder, sharks, even alligators. But what we wanted was catfish. We made a little money selling them, but Dad said it wasn't worth the trouble. He said running the lines is something he used to do with his father. It reminds him of being young. And I suppose every important talk he's ever given me was out there on the calm water, just the two of us, slowly working the fish off the hooks.

I came to the first hook and it was clean. I took it off and dropped it in a small plastic box beside me and pulled to the next one. As the line rose dripping out of the water, I saw a six-pound catfish flipping beneath it. I pulled it into the boat and used the paddle to press it to the deck.

"Careful," Dad said.

"I know," I said.

I removed the hook from its mouth and grabbed the fish so that my fingers went around the fins. Then I dropped it into the cooler and began pulling again.

"Clients canceled on me tonight," he said.

"Because of the storm?"

"Yeah. I figure the least it's gonna do is muddy up this river and flood out the game."

The next hook was empty. I took it off and kept pulling.

"Where do all the animals go?"

"I don't know. I guess most of 'em die. Maybe they get to some high ground somewhere."

I thought about it. All the hogs crowded together on a small piece of ground in the middle of the swamp.

"What's the weirdest thing you ever saw out here?" I asked him.

"What do you mean?" he said.

"Weirdest animal. Anything."

Dad was quiet for a minute. I almost thought he wasn't going to answer.

"I saw a snake one time," he said, "swimmin' the river with a catfish head stickin' out its mouth and the fin stickin' through its back."

"Serious?"

Dad nodded.

"How long you think it was like that?"

The next hook had another, smaller catfish. I worked it off and put it in the cooler.

"I don't know," Dad said. "It's crazy what things can live through."

He got quiet and I worked three more catfish off the line before I spoke again.

"I don't want her to come back, Dad. I wish you'd leave her alone."

"She's your mother."

"I wish it could just be us. I wish she'd move farther away."

"It's complicated, son."

"She said she didn't want you to come over."

"Well, sometimes a woman doesn't know what she wants."

"Why do you do it?"

When I turned to him he was looking away like he didn't want me to see his face. I stopped pulling.

"Dad?" I said.

"Because she's my wife," he said. "Because we're a family."

"All she ever did was complain."

39

He acted like he had to cough and wiped at his face.

"I ain't one to give up on a thing," he said.

"Maybe sometimes you have to."

"Quittin' ain't in my blood, and it ain't in yours," Dad snapped.

I looked down and didn't answer.

I heard him sigh, regretfully. "She wasn't always like that," he said.

I looked up at him again. "But we could be fine," I said. "Just us."

Dad frowned and looked over the river. "You're just gonna have to let me work it out, son . . . I don't wanna talk about it anymore."

We wound up the trotline and took it back to the houseboat. I was busy skinning the catfish on the back deck when Dad passed me without a word, got into his truck, and left. I watched him go, then went inside.

The news showed Igor making landfall in Biloxi. A state of emergency had been declared in Louisiana, Mississippi, Alabama, and Florida. People all along the Gulf Coast were lining up at gas stations and grocery stores to get supplies. Northbound interstates were bumper-to-bumper with a steady flow of traffic headed upstate. About the only vehicles traveling south were the National Guard trucks, loaded with survival supplies and soldiers to guard against looters robbing stores and thieves robbing people's empty houses.

I turned off the television and went back out to finish skinning fish.

9

DAD WAS STILL IN BED WHEN I POURED A BOWL of cereal Sunday morning.

I left the television on and walked outside. Two pickup trucks were backed down the launch ramp, pulling out their boats. I ran my eyes over the stalls and saw that six of them were already empty.

I heard someone walk up behind me and turned to see Dad, rubbing his eyes like he hadn't had any sleep.

"I guess we ought to get after it," he said.

"What do you want me to do?"

"Go over to the shed. I'll meet you there with the truck, and we can load that plywood and take it to the Stovalls'."

As I was crossing the yard I saw the girls up at the house getting into Mrs. Stovall's car for church. Both of them wore matching yellow dresses with green ribbons in their hair. Like two colorful birds on the hill. Liza waved to me and I lifted my hand at her.

We spent all morning hauling the heavy four-by-eight

sheets of half-inch plywood up to the house and screwing them over the windows. It was exhausting work, but I didn't mind. I felt better about everything again, with Dad there and things getting done.

We took a break for lunch and ate peanut butter and jelly sandwiches on the houseboat. The sky was blue and only an occasional breeze rippled the surface of the river. It was hard to imagine the storm I'd seen on the news was out there. Despite the good weather, there was a sense of urgency developing at the landing. More people were arriving to get their boats out of the stalls and the boatyard and take them away to higher ground. Everyone seemed in a hurry and not willing to stay and talk much.

"What do you wanna do about this houseboat?" I asked Dad.

"I'm thinkin' about it."

"We could anchor it up in one of the creeks."

"It'll take more than the two of us to get this thing upriver," he said.

"We gonna stay up at the Stovalls' until the storm's over?"

"Yeah, I guess."

"We need to make sure their generator's working."

"Yeah," he said. "And we still gotta get all our stuff off this thing and haul it up to their garage."

"What about the boats people haven't gotten?"

Dad looked out at the stalls. Then he ran his eyes over the yard.

"Still got two in the slips. Looks like Gant and Blake. They'll be here. Any of those boats left in the yard, they'll have to take their chances they don't get a tree on 'em. I don't think the water's gonna get up there."

Dad stuffed the last bite of his sandwich into his mouth and stood up.

"Let's get on the roof and put some more nails in that sheet tin on the south side. It's gonna get hit the worst."

I crossed the yard again and got the nails and two hammers out of the shed. Dad was already putting the ladder against the roof of the stalls when I returned. We climbed up and started driving extra nails along the seams of the aluminum sheets. I always liked the view of the river from there. You could hear the rush of it and see spoonbills rolling out in the center. The breeze had picked up slightly and tossed my hair about, but it was just a normal, blustery fall afternoon.

At one point I looked up to see the Carters' Suburban coming down the hill. Mr. Carter pulled into the yard and backed up to their flats boat. It was the newest and most expensive boat at the landing, a twenty-two-foot Scout with a 225 Yamaha four-stroke. Even though the boat had a custom canvas cover to protect it from the weather, it bothered me to watch it sitting out in the sun and rain.

"Figured he'd forget about it," Dad said. "I can't remember the last time I saw 'em use it."

I watched Jason Carter get out of the passenger side and direct his father to match their trailer ball to the receiver. Like Liza, he was in my same eighth-grade class at school. In addition to having a father with a lot of money, he was captain of the basketball team and good at just about anything else he was involved in. He was easily the most popular boy in our grade.

Jason looked up and saw me. "How's it going, Cort?"

"Just trying to get ready," I said.

Jason seemed to have everything, including a piece of my life at the landing. But I was okay with him until he asked Liza to the fall dance at our school the year before. Ever since then I'd felt the heat of jealousy creep into my face when I saw him.

"Basketball team's off to a good start this year," he said. "Too bad you can't come out with us."

"Maybe next year," I said.

It burned me up to think that I should have asked her myself. But I didn't. I was scared it would make things weird between us. So I'd stayed home and watched

Mr. Carter's Suburban pull up before her house. I saw Jason go to the door, and she came out in a pretty dress and they took her away like I'd never see her again.

The next day I asked her if she was his girlfriend.

"No," she said, like it was a crazy thought.

And I suddenly realized I didn't want to know any more.

Jason now glanced up at the house. "Liza around?" he asked.

"No."

"Tell her I'll call her," he said.

I nodded at him. He could just roll into anywhere and take what he wanted. And there was nothing I could do about it.

Mr. Carter got their boat connected and they started to get back into their Suburban.

"See you at school," Jason said, "after this thing blows over."

"Yeah," I said. "See you later."

Dad glanced up as the Carters pulled away.

"Maybe your mother can still pick you up from practice. I'll talk to her about it."

"I can't count on her."

"I'd get you myself, but I've got to make a livin'. I'm usually on the river in the afternoons."

"I know," I said. "Forget about it."

*　*　*

That evening I heard tires crunching on the gravel road up the hill. I watched headlights coming down to the river-bank. The car pulled to a stop just above me and I saw it was Sheriff Curly Stanson, Dad's friend since grade school. He left the engine running and stepped out with a cheek full of sunflower seeds. He spit a hull at the dirt and studied me over the roof of the patrol car. His door chime dinged softly against the night.

"Cort," he said.

"Hey, Mr. Stanson."

"Y'all ready for this thing?"

"We're working on it."

"Where's your dad?"

"Up the road, I guess."

The sheriff frowned and spit again. "What you gonna do about this houseboat?"

"I don't know. He said he's thinking about it."

"I hope you don't plan on stayin' on it."

"I think we're gonna stay up at the Stovalls'."

The sheriff nodded considerately.

"Does Tom know the governor issued a mandatory evacuation order?"

"I told him. But we don't have to leave, right?"

"No, but if you get in any trouble, they won't send help. You're on your own."

"I think he knows."

"Okay. Well, it's my job to make sure everybody's aware of the situation."

I nodded.

"Yeah, well, school's canceled. I guess you figured that."

"Yes, sir."

The sheriff spit again. "Okay. I'll be back around tomorrow in case anybody needs help before this mess gets started."

He got back into his patrol car and pulled away. I watched his brake lights come on uphill at the Stovalls' house. I saw him get out and approach their door. I looked down at Catfish. "I guess we might as well get some sleep," I said to him.

I got Catfish settled into an old army blanket on the floor. Then I climbed up top and lay there staring at the ceiling, listening to the creaking of the pontoons and the chatter of the swamp outside. It was hard to imagine that all of it would soon be wind-thrashed and flooded. My gut told me we hadn't prepared enough. We hadn't hauled our stuff out, tested the generator, or even secured the houseboat. It didn't seem possible to get it all done in time.

10

MONDAY MORNING THE HURRICANE WAS STILL A hundred miles away, but I already sensed it. The sky was a gray blanket of clouds easing strangely east to west, and the air was wet and thick. The Tensaw was three feet above the normal high-water mark, heavy and calm and patient. The only noise was that of a few seagulls keeing and flying lazily upriver. Otherwise there wasn't a fish popping the surface, not a leaf trembling, not even a crow calling. The animals felt danger approaching, and their absence left an eerie stillness hanging over the swamp.

It was nearly eight o'clock and Dad was sleeping in again. I stepped off the houseboat and looked over the landing. I heard Francie squeal and turned to see her playing with Catfish near the launch ramp. She saw me and pointed at the dog.

"He won't let Elmo ride!" she said, laughing.

She was trying to put the doll on his back. Catfish moved a few paces away, being patient with her but not willing to play her game.

I crossed the boardwalk onto the riverbank.

"Stay close, Francie," I said. "It's about to storm."

She approached Catfish again and he dodged her once more.

"Sit down," I said. "He'll come up to you."

She sat and put Elmo in her lap, and I started uphill.

Liza opened the door, still in her pajamas. "No school," she announced.

"I know," I said. "Still got a lot of work to do, though."

I followed her into the kitchen. The house was strangely dark and quiet inside with the windows covered. Mrs. Stovall came down the hall with a towel on her head.

"Good mornin', Cort," she said. "Would you like some breakfast?"

"Sure," I said.

"We're movin' a little slow around here today."

"That's okay. So's Dad."

Liza opened the refrigerator and peered into it. "What do you want, Cort?"

"Whatever," I said. "It doesn't matter."

She got out a carton of eggs and a package of bacon and set them on the counter. Mrs. Stovall brushed past her, set the skillet on the stove, and turned on the burner.

"Did you see Francie out there?" Mrs. Stovall asked.

"Yes, ma'am. She's playing with Catfish."

I sat down at the kitchen table and Liza sat across from me.

"I can help get ready today," Liza said. "Whatever we need to do."

"I'll go into town and get some canned food and jugs of water," Mrs. Stovall said. "Anything else?"

"You better get flashlight batteries and some mantles for the propane lanterns. We'll need insect repellant, too."

Mrs. Stovall placed several strips of bacon into the skillet. In a moment it was popping and sizzling. As the savory smell of it filled the kitchen I thought back to cold winter mornings on the houseboat when the windows were glazed over with ice and the propane heaters hissed and warmed the room. It was when Mom was still around and Dad cooked breakfast for the three of us. It had been a long time since I'd seen him cook anything.

After breakfast Mrs. Stovall got her rain jacket off the back of a chair and her purse off the sideboard. I heard rain pattering the roof and a couple of hickory nuts thump and roll off.

"Make sure Francie stays close," she said.

"Okay," I said. "We'll keep an eye on her."

She started out the door and I got up and took my plate

to the sink. Liza came to the counter and started washing the dishes.

"I better go see if Dad's up," I said.

"Okay," she said. "I'll come help after I finish the dishes and get dressed."

"Put on a raincoat," I said. "Sounds like the rain's already here."

11

IT WAS SPRINKLING WHEN I STEPPED OUTSIDE.
Blake Corte's truck was pulling up the ramp, trailering
his pontoon boat from slip seven. I raised my hand at
him, and he lifted a finger off his steering wheel and continued uphill.

There was still one pickup parked below. I saw Francie
by the boat stalls dangling her Elmo doll by the arm. I
walked downhill and found her watching Gant Hartley
getting his jon ready for takeout.

"You got everything under control, Cort?" he asked.

"Getting there," I said. I turned to Francie. "You and
Elmo need to go inside, Francie. Your mom's at the store,
but Liza's up there."

"When's the storm coming, Cort?" she asked.

"Soon," I said.

"Looks like we're runnin' out of time," Mr. Hartley
said.

"Yes, sir," I said. "Go on, Francie."

She turned and ran for the house. Catfish watched her go, then came up against me.

"You need some help with that?" I asked.

"I got it," he said. "You better tend to your houseboat."

"I know. Good luck."

"You, too, Cort. Be safe."

I started back to the houseboat and saw Dad standing on the back porch sipping coffee and studying the river. As I drew close he lowered his cup and looked over at me.

"Looks like we're about to get wet," he said.

"At least they got all the boats out," I said.

"We still got one more. Why don't you run the jon around to the ramp and I'll back the truck down."

I untied the jon and motored to the launch ramp. The rain had turned to a steady drizzle by then. I pulled my cap low over my eyes and waited for Dad. After a few minutes he arrived with the boat trailer. I motored the jon onto the runners and sat in it while he pulled it up the hill. He parked it behind the Stovalls' house beside Mr. Stovall's old center-console. I jumped out and un-hooked the trailer, and he drove back down to the house-boat.

Liza appeared at the back door as I was pulling the drain plug. She wore her hunting boots and a rain jacket with the hood pulled over her head.

"You think a tree's gonna fall on them?" she asked.

"I hope not. Your mom's got to put her car in the garage, so there won't be room for 'em in there."

"Guess it doesn't matter about Dad's," she said, looking at her father's old boat.

"That thing still runs good. We used it a month ago."

She studied it doubtfully.

"Those Evinrude seventies are tough," I said.

"Francie's watching cartoons," she said. "What do you want me to do?"

"I think we're gonna start bringing our stuff up here. Dad's probably down there right now looking at it all."

"Don't you want a raincoat?"

I wore cutoff jeans, tennis shoes, an old T-shirt, and a baseball cap pulled low over my eyes. As much as I had to do, I'd get wet no matter what I wore.

"I'm fine," I said.

For the rest of the morning Dad hauled our fishing equipment, traps, and clothes out of the houseboat and set them on the deck. Liza and I loaded the back of the pickup in the drizzling rain, using a tarp to cover everything and keep it from getting too wet. When the truck bed was full she climbed into the passenger seat and Dad sat on the tailgate. I drove us up to the Stovalls' garage, where the three of us stacked it all inside against the wall.

Mrs. Stovall returned just before noon and told us to come inside for sandwiches. By then the wind was coming in steady gusts over the water oaks and we heard hickory nuts rapping on the tin roof of the bait shop. We had nearly everything in the garage except for our two rifles, which Dad hung on the gun rack in the truck.

"What about the houseboat, Dad?"

"I'm still thinkin' about it," he said. "At least we got just about everything important off it. Still need to get the stuff out of the refrigerator and pack it on ice. Once we lose power it'll all spoil."

Mrs. Stovall brought towels out to the garage, and we dried our heads and faces and took off our wet shoes. When we walked into the kitchen she was making ham and cheese sandwiches for us.

"The stores are out of just about everything," she said. "I had to go all the way to the Dollar General in Bay Minette."

"I still gotta get ice and some gas for that generator," Dad said.

"I already got gas," she said. "It's in the back of my car. I had to wait in line for an hour."

"Glad you thought of that," he said. "Cort'll get those cans out, and we'll make sure the generator works. Hopefully, they'll still have some ice somewhere."

After a quick lunch it was time to go back to work.

"What's next?" Liza asked.

"Why don't you see what flashlights and batteries you

can find, sweetheart," Dad said. "Get those propane lanterns out of the garage and put some new mantles on 'em.
You know how to do that?"

"I know how."

"I can help you," I said.

"Fill 'em with fuel," Dad said. "Linda, fill up your bath-
tubs and washing machine with water so we can use it
when the pump quits. I've got to get started on the houseboat. It's gettin' mean out there."

12

AFTER I HELPED LIZA TIE MANTLES ONTO THE propane lanterns I walked down to the houseboat to see what Dad was doing. The river was already rising steadily under the rain, but there was still no current. The wind gusted across the flat muddy surface like sweeps from a giant broom, and the houseboat creaked and twisted. Catfish stood on the porch watching me.

"Hey!" Dad called out.

I turned to see him standing uphill next to a big water oak.

"Go get those ropes out of the bow. We're gonna tie off to these trees up here."

We spent most of the afternoon slipping in the mud and ducking into the wind and rain, using the heavy one-inch ropes to tie the bow and stern to two water oaks about twenty feet up the riverbank. Then we adjusted the spuds, ten-foot lengths of three-inch galvanized pipe running through iron collars at the four corners of the boat. They hung like skinny legs into the mud to stabilize the platform. We clamped them off at three feet to allow the boat to swing in closer to the bank.

When Dad was satisfied we'd done all we could do with the houseboat, I helped him load our small electric generator into the back of the truck. It wasn't as big as the Stovalls', and wouldn't power much, but we could use it for backup. We hauled it uphill, lugged it into the garage, and set it behind Mrs. Stovall's car.

"Go shut off the water to the bait shop," he told me. "If those pipes break, we don't want water spewin' every-where. And go around the back of the shed and flip those breakers to shut down the power at the stalls so we don't have broken power lines lyin' hot."

I nodded that I understood. Then Liza appeared at the garage door in her raincoat, looking bored.

"Need some more help?" she asked.

Dad started toward the truck. "Find all the extension cords you can and put 'em out here by the generator," he said.

"Okay," she said.

Dad slammed his door against the rain and scratched out in the gravel.

I started into the storm again. "I gotta go back down there," I said over my shoulder. "We're almost done."

"Get Catfish," she called to me.

I waved to her that I'd heard.

What little daylight we had left was fading. I shut off the water and the electricity, then went back down to the houseboat to help Dad load the food from the refrigerator and whatever else was left. We made our final haul up-hill, unloaded it, and returned once more to make a last pass through the boat. Dad stood in the middle of the kitchen floor, studying the empty space. After a moment he flipped a switch to turn on the battery-powered porch lights.

"I guess that's all we can do," he said. "We'll leave these AC lights on so we can watch it. I'll unplug the shore power and drag the line uphill a little ways."

It looked strange with just about everything out except the furniture and appliances. I saw Catfish relaxing on the sofa, muddy and wet and unconcerned.

"Get him up to the house," Dad said. "I'm gonna go see if I can find some ice somewhere."

"You don't think everything's closed by now?"

He looked out the window and eyed the river through the rain like it might have an answer. After a second he turned and started for the door. "I don't know," he said. "We'll see."

I watched Dad walk away and looked down at Catfish. "Come on, boy," I said. "Time to get out of here."

He acted as though he didn't hear me, but I saw his ear twitch.

I glanced about until I saw a rope hanging on the wall. I got it and tied one end to his collar and made a loop for my wrist on the other end.

"You're not gonna like this," I said. "But you can't stay here tonight."

I tugged the rope and he looked at me stubbornly. This houseboat was his home as much as mine, and he hadn't slept anywhere else in years.

"It's for your own good," I said. "Come on."

I tugged the leash again, and he dropped off the sofa and came to me. I pulled him onto the deck and closed the door.

13

LIZA WAS ACTUALLY THE FIRST ONE WHO EVER saw Catfish. She was up in a mulberry tree alongside the riverbank when he came trotting through the woods. I was below picking up berries as she shook them off the tree limbs.

"Dog coming, Cort," she said, like it was nothing unusual.

I turned and saw the dirty yellow mutt stop and study me.

"No collar," I said. "You see his tail wagging?"

"Can't see from here. Go try to pet him."

"Heck, no! He might have rabies or something."

"Well, then, let him pass."

There was something about the way the dog was looking at me that kept me considering it all. He was muddy and had briars tangled in his coat, but there was nothing threatening about him. He reminded me of a mischievous kid coming back from playing in a mud puddle.

"You think I should pet him?" I asked.

"I'm coming down."

I knew Liza would pet a stray dog without thinking twice. And then it would be hers. Suddenly I wanted my own dog more than anything in the world.

"No!" I called up to her. "I'm walking over there."

From then on Catfish followed me everywhere. He was my first friend in the mornings and my last friend in the evenings. He was also the one I talked to about Mom and Dad. I didn't realize things between them were as bad as they were until after Mr. Stovall died. By then the subject of parent problems wasn't anything I felt comfortable talking to Liza about. Catfish was the only one I told everything to. Even if he was just a dog, he made me feel a little less alone in the world.

I remembered Dad telling me to leave the garage door open to ventilate the generator. Besides, once we lost power we might not be able to raise the door. I tied Catfish to the bumper of Mrs. Stovall's car and put out a blanket for him to sleep on. He whined plaintively and refused to lie down. He wanted to be back on the houseboat.

"You'll be all right," I told him.

I dropped my wet clothes on the floor of the garage, toweled off, and got an old pair of khaki shorts and a shirt out of one of the garbage bags. After changing I remembered that we hadn't tested the generator. I got the gas cans out of Mrs. Stovall's car, filled the fuel tank, checked the oil, and yanked the starter cord. It fired on the first pull. I shut it down and backed away. Then I heard someone in the doorway and turned to see Francie.

"You finished, Cort?" she asked me.

I took a deep breath. "Yeah, Francie," I said. "I think so."

"Come play Candy Land," she said.

"I'll be there in a minute," I said.

She turned and went back into the house.

"Cort's finished!" I heard her announce.

I stood there for a moment, staring into the weather. Now it was too dark to see the river, but I could just make out the lights of the houseboat, dull and yellow through the rain. Something didn't look right. The lights weren't level. The houseboat seemed to be leaning. I figured one of the ropes was too short and holding the corner down. If that was the case, the boat would eventually flood, get heavy, and tear loose.

I dug the portable radio out of a dry bag and keyed it.

"Dad?" I said.

I waited for a moment, but there was no answer. I shook my head and clipped the radio to my belt. I went inside to find Liza and Francie starting a game of Candy Land on the living room floor. Mrs. Stovall was in the laundry room folding clothes and letting the washer fill for backup water. Pine limbs scraped the windowpanes, and pine cones and branches thumped the roof.

"You think we're ready?" Liza asked me.

"I don't know," I said. "Dad's gone to get ice for the cooler, but something's not right about the houseboat."

"He should be back soon."

I frowned doubtfully. *Surely he isn't at Mom's now,* I thought. *Not now. Not with all this going on.*

14

AS THE OUTSIDE EDGES OF HURRICANE IGOR TORE
into the Gulf Coast, the four of us sat around the Stovalls'
kitchen table, listening to the giant storm spitting rain
and tossing the trees.

"He should have been back a long time ago," I said.

"Try to call him again."

I shook my head. "He's not answering."

"Maybe he got blown away," Francie said.

Mrs. Stovall got up from the table. "Francie," she said.
"It's bedtime."

"But what if he got blown way up into a tree?"

"He didn't get blown away. Now, go back to your
room and I'll be there in a minute to tuck you in."

Francie disappeared down the hall, dragging Elmo.

"Maybe everybody's out of ice," Liza said.

"He's up at Mom's . . . You know that."

"Maybe it's best if she has someone with her,"
Mrs. Stovall said.

"I think the houseboat's already hung up, and I can't move it by myself."

Mrs. Stovall walked over to the television and watched the weather report for a moment.

"It looks like we've still got a couple of hours before it gets really bad," she said. "This is just the edge of it."

"He should be here with us," I said.

Mrs. Stovall took a deep breath and let it out. "Let me get Francie to bed," she said. "Then I'll go get him. It shouldn't take me more than fifteen minutes. And your mom can come back over here if she wants."

I didn't care about avoiding Mom anymore. Now Dad was endangering the Stovalls, and for the first time my frustration turned to anger.

"You shouldn't have to do that," I said.

"If I'm goin', I need to go now before it gets much worse," she said.

I rethought it all, trying to make sure I wasn't being overly concerned. But there was definitely something wrong with the boat. And if we lost it, we'd be in big trouble.

"Okay," I said. "You better go."

Mrs. Stovall went to tuck Francie in bed. She returned a few minutes later, got her rain jacket and a flashlight, and headed for the door.

"Watch out for Catfish," I said. "He's tied behind your car."

"I'll move him," she said.

"Be careful, Mom," Liza said.

I had a bad feeling about Mrs. Stovall leaving, but I had an even worse feeling about going through the storm without Dad.

After Mrs. Stovall was gone, Liza and I watched the news on television. The eye of the storm was only a few hours from landfall, and the weatherman was making his report from a beach somewhere in the midst of it. He ducked into his microphone, his rain suit flapping in the gale-force winds, tremendous dirty waves smashing into a seawall behind him.

An hour passed before the phone rang again. Liza answered it. "Okay," she said. "We'll stay inside. No, she's still asleep. Okay. I love you, too. We will."

She held the phone out to me. "Your dad wants to talk to you."

"Hey," I said into the phone.

"Y'all doin' all right?"

"Right now we are."

"Listen, the creek's already up over the bridge. We can't get back there. Looks like you're in charge."

"Why didn't you answer your radio?"

"Battery's dead. You can call us here."

"At Mom's?"

"Yeah."

I took a deep breath. "Dad, I'm worried about the houseboat. It's not floating right, and the river's still rising."

"We've done all we can do about that," he said.

"I feel like I should cut one of the lines and pull the spuds."

"Just stay away from it. It's too dangerous to cut the lines if they're strained like that."

"I don't know how to wire the generator into the electrical panel."

"Don't worry about that. If you lose power, just plug some lights and the deep freeze into an extension cord. Keep the refrigerator door shut as much as you can, and it'll stay cool for a while."

More questions spun in my head as Dad hung silently on the other end of the line. It seemed none of this was a big deal at all to him. Then I realized I would never be able to ask him all I needed to know. And the phones were probably going to go dead. Anger suddenly flooded over me and I couldn't hold it back.

"Dad, I just want you back here! Why aren't you here?"

"I meant to be, son. I just got behind. Your mother's by herself and—"

"She's a grown-up, Dad! We're kids! What if something happens to the houseboat? What are we gonna do then?"

"Calm down, son. You can do this. You got a better head on your shoulders than your old man. You just need to use it and keep everybody safe."

I stared at the floor, breathing out my anger, trying to calm myself.

"Cort?"

"What?" I snapped.

"Don't worry about it. You'll be fine."

"I don't know *how*."

"Just stay inside and use your head."

I rubbed my face and sighed. "There's no way you can make it back?"

"We'll get over there tomorrow as soon as we can."

"Okay," I said.

"Call me if you need me," Dad said.

"Charge your radio," I said, "before the power goes out."

"All right," he said. "I will."

I hung up the phone and stood there staring at it.

"Mom's worried," Liza said.

"Yeah, me too . . . But we'll just stay inside. Go check on Francie. Don't tell her about your mom being gone."

Liza disappeared down the hall and I turned to the television again. The hurricane was already using its eastern-flank winds to blow the Gulf water directly into Mobile Bay and up into the rivers and swamps. The weatherman said we were on the eastern side of the eye wall and would receive the worst of it. The water would continue to rise, and the wind and rain would increase. Once the eye passed, the wind would shift and start blowing from the west. Then Igor would turn and move northeast, crossing the head of the Mobile-Tensaw Delta. It would continue to dump rain into the river systems, prolonging the floodwater to the south. Even after the storm passed upstate, the floodwater would last for days. And our parents weren't going to be back any time soon.

15

LIZA RETURNED FROM FRANCIE'S ROOM AND I switched off the television. We'd both seen enough. There was nothing left to do but stay inside and hope for the best.

"How's she doing?" I asked.

"She's fine. I told her she could sleep with me."

"You give her that little flashlight?"

"She's got it next to her."

Liza went to their bookshelf and pulled down a Monopoly game.

"You want to play?" she asked me.

"I guess," I said.

I sat across from her on the floor as she stacked the cards and arranged the money. I suddenly realized that I was going to be alone with her all night, and things weren't so bad anymore. I studied her face, thinking how pretty she was. I wondered what she really thought about me. *She is so much better than me,* I thought. *She'll have*

*boyfriends like Jason. She'll never have a boyfriend who
lives on a houseboat.*

She finished sorting the money and looked up. "You
want to be the car again?"

"Okay," I said.

She got the car and put it on the board. Then she got
the hat for herself.

"Do you think it's weird to live on a houseboat?" I
asked her.

She looked at me. "I think it's kind of cool."

"But what if you were older? Would you want to live
on one?"

"I don't know."

"Sometimes I wish I just had a regular house," I said.

"One day you can."

She picked up the dice and rolled them on the board.
I watched her face.

"You remember when we found those flying squirrels?" I said.

Liza smiled. "I remember. You wanted to keep one for
a pet, but we couldn't catch them."

"We tried all day."

"They were too big."

"Yeah," I said. "I think you have to get 'em when
they're babies."

"You found Catfish," she said.

"*You* did, really."

"I saw him, but he liked you best."

"He likes you, too."

Liza moved the hat to the Just Visiting square. "Visiting jail," she said. "Boring. Your roll."

"Do you still wanna leave?"

"What?"

"Leave here. One time you said you wanted to move away."

"That was a long time ago."

"But you never said you changed your mind."

Liza studied the board, but I could see she wasn't thinking about Monopoly.

"And you don't come down to the river much anymore," I said.

"It's different now," she said.

"But your family's had this place for a long time."

She looked at me. "My family's not here anymore. At least not all of it."

I felt the stab of her answer. I knew what she was saying without her really having to say it.

"But how would moving help?"

I saw she didn't want to answer me. She didn't have to. Suddenly we heard a loud boom and a crash. The lights flickered and went out.

16

WE SAT IN COMPLETE DARKNESS, LISTENING TO the storm batter the house.

"I guess that's it," I said.

Liza reached out and touched my arm. "I can't see anything," she said.

"Momma!" Francie yelled from the back bedroom.

"It's okay," Liza called to her. "I'm coming. Turn on your flashlight."

I stood. "I've got another one on the counter," I said. "Let me feel my way to it, and I'll get the generator going."

I found the flashlight, went out to the garage, and started the generator. I plugged up an extension cord and walked the end of it back inside. Liza was standing in the middle of the floor, holding Francie by the hand.

"See," she said to her. "Cort's getting the lights on."

"Where's Momma?" Francie asked.

"She had to go check on Mrs. Delacroix."

"When's she coming back?"

"We can call her if you want."

"I wanna call her."

"Hold on, Francie," I said. "I'll get the phone working in just a minute."

On the kitchen counter was a power strip. I attached it and plugged in the freezer and two lamps. Then I plugged in the phone base and gave Liza the handset.

"You know the number?" she asked.

"No," I said. "Check the caller ID."

Liza found the number, called it, got her mother on the line, and told her we were okay. Then she let Francie talk, and whatever their mother said calmed Francie.

I got the propane lanterns, lit them, and took one to each of the back bedrooms. By the time I got to Liza's room she was in bed with Francie, reading a storybook to her with a flashlight. I put a lantern on the bedside table. Francie eyed it and eased deeper under the covers.

"You like that?" I said.

She smiled and nodded.

"Like camping out."

"Thanks," Liza said.

"I'm going back to the garage to check on Catfish and look at the houseboat."

"He needs some food," Francie bossed.

I smiled at her. "Okay," I said. "I'll get him something."

* * *

Catfish was standing and staring anxiously into the storm when I found him. Mrs. Stovall had retied him to the tracks of the garage door, and he was straining at the end of the leash, nearly in the rain. In the distance I saw the houseboat lights glowing dull and yellow.

"What you see out there, boy?"

He whined and continued studying the darkness. I got his dog food out of one of the garbage bags and poured it into a bowl for him.

"Come on," I said.

But he was more interested in whatever he saw beyond the garage lights. I set the food down and approached him. I knelt and scratched his neck and stared into the static of wind and rain. As my eyes adjusted I saw the vague silhouette of a doe standing still as a statue. I'd never seen a deer that close to the house. She seemed stricken with confusion.

"I see it," I said.

Catfish strained at the leash and trembled and whined.

It suddenly occurred to me that the animals were being driven from the swamp. Deer, wild hogs, bears—everything. There was no telling what was out there. They were all fleeing for their lives.

17

IT WAS CLOSE TO NINE-THIRTY AND NONE OF US
were sleeping. The storm continued to pound on the house
like it wanted to get at us. Francie was still up watching
cartoons in the back bedroom. Liza was reading a book
and I was catching a catnap on the floor. The generator
hammered away in the garage, lighting our storm shelter,
giving us a small sense of security.

"What was the deer doing?" Liza asked me.

"It was just standing there. Like it was confused."

"How many do you think will drown?"

"I don't know. Prob'ly a lot. I remember after the last
hurricane there were dead animals floating in the river
for a week. Until the alligators ate 'em all."

"Maybe—"

We heard breaking glass followed by Francie screaming. I jumped up and rushed toward Liza's bedroom.
Francie collided with me in the hall and I picked her up
and held her.

"What happened, Francie?"

She was too hysterical to answer. Liza came up and took her from me and went back to the living room, talking softly to her.

I walked into the bedroom and saw a pine limb jammed through the curtains and wet glass splinters glistening on the carpet. Rain was running down the wall. I returned to the girls and found Liza on the sofa, holding and rocking Francie. In place of her pajamas Francie had on a T-shirt and tiny jeans with red hearts sewn onto the pockets. Her flashlight was peeking out from one of them.

"It's just a broken windowpane," I said. "Tree branch punched through the plywood."

"It's just a broken window," Liza whispered to her.

"I'm scared," Francie said.

"It's okay," Liza said. She looked at me and rolled her eyes. "She says she's not going to bed. So she got dressed."

"I want Momma," Francie said.

"She's not back yet, Francie," Liza said.

"I don't wanna go to sleep," Francie said.

"That's fine," I said. "You can stay out here with us."

"What's gonna happen to us?"

"Nothing," I said. "It's just a little wind and rain."

"Is Catfish okay?"

"He's fine," I said. "Don't worry about him."

"I wanna go see him."

I looked at Liza. She didn't object.

"You can go see him," I said. "Just stand by the door and talk to him."

Francie got up and started toward the garage.

Liza looked at me.

"If she just stands by the door, she won't get wet," I said.

Liza stood. "I better go with her."

I got duct tape and a plastic garbage bag out of the kitchen and returned to the bedroom with them. I slipped on my sneakers and crunched through the glass and shoved the pine limb outside. Then I took off my shirt and used it to protect my hands as I picked the jagged remains of the windowpane from the frame. I spent the next twenty minutes taping the garbage bag over the hole and cleaning up the glass on the floor. When I was done I walked back into the kitchen and started shaking my shirt over the sink.

"Cort!" I heard Liza shout.

I dropped the shirt and bolted for the garage. I ran into Liza in the hallway. She was soaking wet and her eyes were wide with terror.

"Catfish ran off! Francie's wrist got caught in the leash!"

"Where is she?"

"Out there! I can't see her! I can't hear her, Cort!"

18

I RAN STRAIGHT OUT INTO THE STORM.

"Francie!" I yelled.

The wind swept my voice away like tissue paper. Liza ran up behind me and put her hand on my shoulder. I turned to her and saw her face rain-streaked and horrified.

"I'm going down there!" I yelled to her.

She clung to my arm. I heard cracking and snapping and the tremendous crash of a tree from somewhere below.

"Go back inside!" I shouted.

Liza shoved me ahead. There was no time to argue. I shielded my eyes and started downhill, trying to see the lights of the houseboat. I didn't look back, but I knew Liza was following me. The wind gusted and the rain stung my bare skin like cold lead shot. I couldn't see anything, but I could find my way through the darkness on memory. What squeezed at my gut was the fact that

I should have been able to see the lights of the boat. And they weren't there.

I turned to Liza. She was a vague silhouette only a few feet behind. "Go back and get a light!" I yelled.

"Cort!"

"Go!"

She turned and disappeared.

I continued downhill until my shoes slapped into cool water. I thought it was impossible to be at the river so soon. I took another step and the water was up to my shins. I looked up and saw the outline of the treetops against the sky glow. My mind raced to reference it, but everything was twisted and moving and not like I remembered. I ran blindly along the water's edge looking for the boat. Suddenly I crashed into a muddy, gnarled mass of tree roots and slipped into a depression of wet clay. I fought my way out of the hole and around it to find the trunk of a fallen water oak disappearing into black water. I immediately looked up and saw the top of the second oak waving and tossing not far from me. I hopped the fallen trunk and splashed to the second tree, feeling for the rope, waiting for it to clip me in the stomach.

"Francie!" I yelled.

I thought I heard a faint cry just before the rope cut against my chest tight as a cable. I grabbed it and rushed into the water, pulling myself toward whatever it held.

"Francie!"

I heard her scream.

"Don't move!"

Several yards out from the bank I felt the river current pulling on me. I lost my footing and continued on arm strength alone.

The rope suddenly lost its tension. I didn't know why. I was still pulling myself through the current when I heard a wet, oily, cracking sound. A moment later something hit me across the back like a baseball bat, tore the rope from my hands, and pressed me straight down against the river bottom. I was suddenly repositioned in a swirl of liquid darkness. It seemed everywhere I moved, I came up against a tangle of vines and limbs. I kicked my shoes off and swiped and twisted my way toward the surface. When I broke the water I was in the midst of the treetop. I grabbed and pulled my way through it.

"Francie!"

I didn't hear an answer. I kept fighting my way clear of the tree branches until I felt the river current swirling around me. I was disoriented. I didn't know where the rope was. I suppressed the fear and was able to reason that I needed to find my way back to the base of the tree, find the rope again, and start over. Going by the way the current was moving, I instinctively started pulling myself in a direction I felt was the riverbank. In a moment the current was gone and I kicked down and felt mud under-foot. I stood and crashed through the shallows.

"Cort!" I heard Liza yell.

I saw her flashlight yellow and dull through the rain. I ran up against the tree and crawled along it until I felt the rope. I stood with it, limp in my hands. I thought maybe the tree had fallen on the houseboat and had it pinned. I reeled the line frantically until a loose end came flipping whiplike into my face.

I dropped the rope and felt my belt for the radio. It was gone.

"Cort!" Liza yelled again.

I ran past her. "Go call Dad!" I yelled.

"I tried! The phone's out!"

My mind raced. "Go wait at the ramp! The houseboat's loose! Francie's on it!"

19

I SLIPPED AND FELL ON THE HILLSIDE, CLAWED MY way up, and sprinted for the house. I grabbed the tongue of our boat trailer and pulled it out the driveway. Then I shoved it backward down the gravel road toward the ramp. As it picked up speed I ran behind, holding on to it, until it got ahead of me and I fell face-first, the wet rocks tearing into my face. The boat and trailer plunged into the darkness below. I scrambled to my feet again and went after it. I soon found the boat again, still on the trailer but lodged against a cypress tree and partway in the water.

"Liza!" I yelled.

I leaned into the boat and rocked it up onto its side with strength I'd never had before. Liza appeared next to me and got under it. We lifted until the back end was propped on the tree. Then I ran to the front and pushed. It slid off the trailer and slapped into the water.

"Get in!" I yelled.

She climbed into the front and I crashed through the

water and rolled over the gunnels into the stern. There was water up to my ankles. I remembered the drain plug was out and leaned over and felt around till I found it and crammed it home. Then I squeezed the fuel bulb three times and turned the key. The engine roared to life and I slammed the gearshift into reverse and swung out into the current.

"Get the light out of the dry box!"

I felt the water in turmoil beneath us, twisting and sucking in all directions at once. I shoved the gearshift forward and found the gap in the trees that told me where the main channel was. I flooded the engine with fuel and raced straight out into the river.

"Light!" I yelled again. "In that box!"

Liza knew what to do. She found the spotlight and plugged it into the power outlet on the bow. Suddenly we had a white beam cutting through the rain, over the black swirl of water. We were fully exposed to the winds moaning across the trees and down into the river channel. The boat vibrated and shuddered, and it occurred to me the storm might just lift us like a magnolia leaf and bowl us into the trees. The boat hit something and veered right. I thought about life vests, but I didn't want to waste time. Liza waved the light over a massive tree as it slid by us like a passing ship.

"Keep it on the riverbank! To the left!"

The river was strewn with silent, floating trees, their root systems standing torn and jagged against the light. Hitting any of them would flip us or tear a hole in the hull. I raced past them, going twice as fast with the current. Even then, the boat felt sluggish, like a wet mattress. Then I felt the water splashing around my calves and I knew we were still flooding. And the water was coming too much too fast for just catching rain.

Liza passed the light across the surface ahead. I started to yell at her to keep it against the bank, but then I saw a faint slash of white in the middle of the river.

"There!" I said.

She'd seen it, too. She jerked the beam back again. I rammed my palm against the throttle to get every bit of speed I could and veered toward what appeared to be the roofline of the houseboat.

As we drew closer I was certain it was the houseboat. The weak battery-operated lights glowed from the windows. But I didn't see Francie on the deck. It was like a ghost vessel in the night.

It seemed to take an eternity to close the gap. When we finally came alongside I slammed the jon boat into the pontoons. Liza reached out and held the railing as the back end of the jon swung into the current, aiming to wrench us apart. I scrambled to the bow, grabbed the painter, and rolled over the railing.

"I can't hold it!" she yelled.

"Get out!"

She got to her knees and I pulled her onto the deck. I made some quick wraps around a support column with the rope. Liza scrambled past me as the jon pulled tight and I knotted the line. When I turned I saw her through the window, falling through the front door, Francie rushing into her arms.

I finished tying the line and ran around to the girls. Francie was screaming hysterically, her clothes wet and muddy and torn. Catfish stood in the middle of the floor with a *What now?* look. Then I felt one of the trees bump the pontoons and rock us gently. I realized that we didn't have much time to get out of there. If the boat didn't get crushed against the bank, we'd eventually crash into the cement highway bridge downriver.

20

"WE'VE GOT YOU," LIZA SAID, TRYING TO CALM
Francie. "Everything's gonna be okay."

"I couldn't get back," Francie cried.

"I know," I said. "It's okay. Now we have to get into
life vests. Liza, go get them out of the bow."

Liza began to pull away, but Francie screamed and
clung to her.

"Come on, Francie," I said. "We need to hurry."

Liza picked her up and carried her to the front storage
compartment where we kept the flotation vests.

I have to slow us, I thought. *That will buy time to bail
the jon and get us off this boat.*

I hurried out and ran to each corner of the deck,
dropping the spuds. They fell through their sleeves and
slammed on their caps at a full drop, touching nothing. I
rushed to the bow, dug out the anchor, and heaved it over.
I held the rope as it raced through my hand. When it was
taut I tugged it. Nothing. All of it—spuds and anchor—
dragging under us in liquid space.

I rushed into the generator closet and got a five-gallon paint bucket and ran with it back to the jon. One of the giant trees had its root system against it, nosing it like a whale. The force was deceptive. I looked at the painter, pulled tight, dripping with tension. The support column it was fastened to slowly bowed and creaked and flexed. I took a step back. Suddenly the column exploded outward, tearing part of the roof away with it. The tree swung around and over the jon, pressing it beneath the surface, passing away into the darkness, dragging the boat beneath it.

I turned to see Liza, watching wide-eyed through the window. Francie clung to her leg, frozen with fright. They both had their life vests on.

I hurried inside.

"What do we do now, Cort?" Liza said.

I didn't have an answer. On the kitchen table was another life vest Liza had pulled out for me. I grabbed it, put my arms through it, clicked the fasteners, and cinched it tight. Lying on the counter was a small compass. It occurred to me that I had nothing on me, not even a watch. I grabbed the compass and shoved it into my pocket.

"I dropped the spuds and put out the anchor," I said. "We'll float across shallow water eventually."

"Then what?"

"I don't know yet."

"We can't swim in that river," she said. "It's too swift."

I went past her and into my berth. I dragged the mattress off the bed and pulled it past them.

"Cort, we—"

The floor went from under us and I was in the air. I came down on the kitchen table, which gave way and dropped me to the floor. I rolled over and saw Liza and Francie lying in the hallway. Then there was a hesitation as the river built pressure against the pontoons. The houseboat groaned with torque. Seconds later there came a staggered cracking followed by the sound of splintering wood. The boat jerked forward again and I knew the spuds were gone.

"Everybody okay?" I yelled.

Francie began crying again in a strange, exhausted way. Liza gathered her into her lap and didn't answer me. The houseboat moaned, and we felt the river current swinging us sideways into whatever we'd run into. I rushed outside as the boat settled against a thin stand of hackberry. The river pressed on the up-current pontoon, trying to drive us over or under the obstruction. The houseboat tilted precariously. It was inevitable that it would capsize or get piled on with trees.

I looked at Catfish watching me from above. "Come on, boy," I said.

He took a step back and whined plaintively. He didn't want any part of our plan.

"Catfish," I urged. But I knew I was telling him good-bye more than arguing with him. The floodwater was going to be over his head and he'd have nowhere to get out of it. I already had Francie to carry, and whatever lay ahead was going to be hard enough for Liza without the burden of a frantic, wet dog.

"We've got to go, friend," I said. "I'm sorry."

Another tree bumped and rocked the boat. There was no more time for goodbyes.

"Come on!" I yelled to the girls. "Let's go!"

Liza picked Francie up and hurried onto the deck. Catfish whined and trembled at the sight of us leaving.

"Catfish!" Francie yelled.

"He won't come," I said. "We have to leave him."

"Cort," Liza said.

"He'll die out there, Liza. His best chance is to stay afloat as long as he can."

"No, Cort!" Francie cried.

Liza gave me a horrified look, but she knew I was right. "It's okay, Francie," she said. "He'll be able to swim back. He'll be waiting for us when we get home."

"Francie," I said. "Do you have your flashlight?"

She didn't answer me. I took her from Liza and ran my hands over her wet jeans. Her tiny jeans with the red hearts sewn into them. It gave me some relief to feel the small light still in her pocket.

I held Francie under one arm. "I've got you," I said to her.

I used my free arm to pull my way to the up-side of the boat. Then I climbed over the railing with her and leaped into darkness. I fell into the marshy shallows and pulled Francie to my chest. If she made a sound at all I couldn't hear her over the wind and rain and swirling of the river. I staggered to my feet just as Liza landed beside us. The water was up to my waist and threatening to pull my legs from under me, but there was solid ground underfoot.

"You okay?" I said back to Liza.

"Yes," she said.

I shifted Francie under my arm and plunged forward into a tangle of vines and palmetto.

"Stay right behind me," I said.

"I'm good," she said. "Go."

21

WE WADED ABOUT FIFTY YARDS INTO THE SWAMP before I stopped. The thin canopy of hackberry whipped and thrashed overhead, but the noise was less and the rain no longer stung our faces. Floodwater still pulled at our legs, but among the trees we at least had something to cling to. For the first time in an hour I felt like I had a moment to think.

I can get us out of this.

I gave Francie back to Liza. She held her while I dug the flashlight from her jeans and hoped that it worked. It did. I got the compass from my pocket and held it under the light.

"Cort?" Liza said.

"I'm working on it," I said. "We're gonna be okay now—just let me think."

Think.

I studied the compass, turning and shaking it to make sure it gave a true reading. I didn't believe what it was telling me, but I knew better than to doubt it. We were on the west side of the Tensaw. We had three choices: swim the river, stay where we were, or head west into the swamp. Never in my life had I wished more that Dad was with me. He would know what to do. He would know how to get us to safety.

Finally I said, "We can't swim that river. And the water's still coming up, so we can't stay where we are. We've got to head west into the swamp and get to high ground."

"Where?"

I brought up a mental image of the delta and the river systems that ran veinlike through it. Now that I had a compass reading, I could roughly estimate our location.

Where, Dad? I said to myself. Of course he wasn't there, but it helped a little to pretend he was. And it got me imagining his answers.

"Where, Cort?" Liza said again. "Come on, you know this place."

In my mind I saw nothing but miles of empty marsh. I saw the Mobile River at the edge of that, more swollen and dangerous than the Tensaw. But there was *one* place.

"Bottle Creek," I said. "We'll get up on the Indian mounds."

"How far is that?"

"Prob'ly about a mile, maybe a mile and a half, west of here."

"We can't make that, Cort."

95

"There's nothing else," I said. "You'll have to carry Francie. I need to watch the compass."

Suddenly, Francie wailed sharply and I turned the flashlight on her. She began to squirm and thrash against Liza.

"What's wrong?" I said.

Liza dropped her into the water, jerked off her life vest, and beat it against a tree. Then I saw what was left of the velvety raft of ants floating past us. I grabbed Francie's arm and pulled her to me. I peeled her shirt over her head and brushed my hands over her chest, back, and face. As I did this I felt ants crawling up my ribs and biting me. I lifted Francie from the water and draped her over my shoulder while I brushed at myself.

"It's okay," I told her. "I got 'em off."

She stopped sobbing and lay over my shoulder. I held the light on her shirt while Liza took it from me and turned it inside out and beat the last of the ants from it. Then she took Francie from me again.

"You think it's better on or off?" I asked Liza.

"On," she said. "It's wet, but it's something against the cold. We're gonna get cold."

"I know," I said. "I'm already cold."

She slipped the shirt over Francie's head and snapped her back into the vest.

"Keep her out of the water as much as you can," I said.

Liza didn't answer. I studied the compass. I located

west, looked at the canopy, and found the farthest visible treetop in that general direction. I memorized the pattern of the branches against the sky and set out for it.

The swamp was a tangled mass of wet vines and palmetto and briars, whipped and rain-slashed beneath tall cypress and water oak. It took all my concentration to fight my way forward, keep checking on our direction, and make sure Liza and Francie were behind me. In addition to our struggles against the thick underbrush, the swamp had changed into a place I was no longer familiar with. Everything typically hidden in the damp leaves was climbing into the trees. There were eyes watching us from everywhere. I had a bad feeling that we were going to be up against more than just rising water.

22

"CORT," LIZA SAID.

I stopped and turned to her. The water was two inches higher on her waist than I remembered.

"Is she okay?" I asked.

I ran the light over Francie. She had her eyes open, but she stared back at me in a blank way. Then I put the light on Liza and saw her slumping with exhaustion.

"Let me take her," I said.

I reached out and got Francie in my arms. I patted her on the back and rubbed her shoulders. "I'm gonna take us to my tree fort, Francie. We're gonna wait out the storm in it."

She didn't answer me.

"Let's keep going," Liza said anxiously.

I heard something sigh heavily to my right. I swung the light to find a two-hundred-pound hog standing up to its chin in the floodwater. It was turned sideways to us, its eyes dark and blank. Two tusks protruded from its mouth the color of smokers' yellowed teeth. Wild hogs were good swimmers. I wondered why it was just standing there, letting the water rise over it.

Maybe it's tired, I thought. *Maybe it has given up.*

As if in answer, the hog turned and moved ahead of us into the darkness.

"What was it?" Liza asked.

I moved the light away and gave it to her. "A pig," I said. "It's gone. Can you work the compass?"

She nodded.

"Keep the needle on west."

She put the light on the hog again. I passed her the compass, and she moved ahead of me and stopped and got her bearings.

"Make sure the needle's not stuck," I said.

In a moment she brushed a vine from her face and started forward.

Deep into the swamp the current was gone. There was just flat, endless, rising water. I carried Francie before me, cradled in my arms. She was limp and quiet, but I felt her stomach rising and falling against my own.

I didn't have a watch. I'd kicked my shoes off earlier in the struggle with the houseboat. I wasn't wearing anything now except the old cut-off khakis. The girls didn't have shoes either, but at least their shirts would be a little protection against the cold hard rain. Liza also had a watch, but I didn't see the point in asking what time it was. That would just slow us down.

An explosion of water to the left caused Liza to divert the light, and we caught glimpses of deer leaping and crashing away with their tails standing like white handkerchiefs in the silvery rain. Then I saw her light go down to the compass again, and we pressed on.

I guessed it was close to midnight when she stopped once more. I came up behind her and saw the opening in the trees and the windswept lake beyond. It all looked different, but I knew what we were seeing. For the first time since leaving the boat I had a real landmark. We weren't where I wanted to be, but it could have been much worse.

"Jug Lake," I said. "We've got to head south, then west again."

"How far off are we?"

"It's not bad," I said. "We're close. Bayou Jessamine is in front of us. We don't need to cross that."

"South," she confirmed.

"Yes. What time is it?"

She looked at her wrist. "Twelve-thirty."

"Okay," I said. "Keep going."

Both of us were calmer now, even though the water was another six inches up my stomach. We'd made progress, and that was encouraging. As she moved the light to the compass, it passed over the reflective eyes of something small and furry in a tree. She didn't see it or didn't care. I guessed it was a rat. Something out of place, perched as high as it had to be. I imagined if we took time to study our surroundings we'd see that the trees were stacked with eyes.

Liza led us south. Twice we came against Bayou Jessamine, stopping at the edge of the tree gap and backing away to adjust our course. Sometimes I said Francie's name hoping just to hear her reply. She never answered, but she shifted in my arms and that was enough. Eventually Liza angled west again and I thought about the next obstacle we approached. The bayou we'd been skirting was only twenty feet wide. It would eventually intersect Bottle Creek, and we'd face nearly a hundred feet of water to get across. Normally we could swim it, but if the current was bad, getting to the other side was going to be a big problem.

I didn't say anything to Liza about my concerns. I wouldn't have to. She'd see for herself soon enough. I looked up into the trees, studying their trunks as best I could in the darkness. It was all hackberry and cypress, any limbs that would support us high above the floor.

Getting into them would be like climbing a telephone pole, little to cling to even if we managed to get high enough. And there was no telling what was up there. Everything in the swamp wanted to get into those trees.

But it was the animals that *couldn't* get into the trees that worried me. There was a limited amount of high ground that would remain above the floodwater, and I'd likely be fighting them for it. I wasn't concerned with the deer. It was the hogs I was scared of.

23

GUIDING WILD-HOG HUNTS WAS A LARGE PART OF
Dad's business. Like the alligators, there are too many
hogs, and they've become a problem. Herds of them, with
boars as big as three hundred pounds, roam the marsh,
destructive, violent, and unpredictable.

Dad told me the wild hogs were the descendants of
pigs Hernando de Soto brought into Florida nearly four
hundred years ago. They weren't much of a problem until
the 1980s, when people trucked them across state lines
and released them for hunting. Hogs can live just about
anywhere because they aren't picky about what they eat.
They mostly browse on grass, roots, and stems, but they
also feed on any kind of meat. I've seen them eat arma-
dillos, small deer, snakes, and other hogs. In most places
their only natural predators are panthers and alligators.
There are few panthers left, and gators won't stray far
from the water. Add to this a female hog with as many as
twelve piglets a year, and it's easy to see how they spread
all over the South.

There was no closed season on hogs. Hunters can kill as many as they want, any time of year, day or night. But the permanently open season still isn't enough. Wild hogs aren't just good survivalists—they're smart. It doesn't take long for them to figure out where and how they're being hunted and avoid those places and tactics. That's what makes the delta such a popular destination for hunters. There are thousands of wild pigs in the remote areas of the swamp, and most of them have never seen a man before.

Even though hog hunting is steady business, it's a sport Dad and I don't enjoy being part of. It draws men who are more into cruelty than challenges. They typically use at least two dogs, one to trail the prey and one to "catch" it. The trailing dog, or "chase" dog, can be a redbone or other common baying hound. The catch dog is the thug of the two, a scarred, callous killer. Typically a pit bull, known for its locking bite and instincts to clamp, hold, and shake its prey.

Initially the bay dogs find the pack, single out a big boar, and chase it until it's tired and cornered. The catch dog will then rush the pig until it can get its jaws clamped on the pig's ear and twist it to the ground. It will try to hold the pig in this way until the hunter catches up to the fight.

Most people assume it's a hog's curling yellow tusks

on the top jaw that are dangerous. But the tusks are thick and dull from constant digging into the soil. The cutter teeth on the bottom jaw are what they use to tear flesh. These are two smaller teeth, protruding above and behind each tusk. The hog grinds its tusks against them so they stay sharp enough to shave a fingernail.

The danger lies not only in getting slashed by the cutter teeth but also in catching a sharp hoof to the face or arm. The dogs are often gored or killed in the fight. I've seen them back away with their cheeks hanging open or their intestines hanging from their belly, blue and bloody and leaf-pasted.

While alligators can be deadly, they're easy to avoid. Dad and I have to be more careful around deadly animals that roam on land. We're out there walking around in the dense underbrush most of the year. Dad's always more wary of poisonous snakes than anything else. He has a recurring dream where he's walking barefoot through the swamp and steps on a cottonmouth. He feels the lump of it under his heel like a mushy stick. He's stepped on the middle of it, and it continues to arc its head up and bite his calf. While I don't like snakes either, I have more nightmares about hogs.

When I was ten years old Dad pulled up to the creek bank to let me get out of the boat and pick some muscadine grapes. I hadn't wandered far into the palmetto when I was suddenly charged by a large sow. She bowled me over, bit onto my thigh, and shook me like a doll. It happened so fast that I didn't have time to react. Dad was quick to fire a shot into the air with his rifle. This startled the sow, and I saw her bolt off with a litter of piglets trailing her. I still have the scars from where her teeth punctured my leg. I learned firsthand that wild pigs won't hesitate to attack. And kill you. And eat you.

24

LIZA STOPPED AND I FELT DREAD SLIP OVER ME as I anticipated what lay ahead. I came up beside her and saw the black water of Bottle Creek at her feet.

"Take her," I said.

Liza took Francie and passed me the light and the compass. I shoved the compass into my pocket. Then I put the light on the creek and over it and up into the rain where I couldn't see the opposite bank. I pulled it back to us and upstream, watching the way the water rested against the trees. The current didn't appear to be a serious threat.

"We've got to swim this to get to the mounds," I said.

We still had on our life vests, and Liza was a good swimmer. I wasn't worried about her. I shoved the flashlight into my pocket and took Francie again and held her out before me. "Francie?" I said.

She looked at me.

"You're gonna have to hold on to my neck, okay? I'm gonna have to swim with you on my back."

She stared at me blankly, her lips quivering. I lowered her into the water until she was floating in her vest. Then I crouched and pulled her around behind me. I heard her breathing increase and felt her arms clasp my neck, and I was certain she understood.

"Stay close enough to touch me," I told Liza. "If you start to drift off, grab on to my vest. I can pull us all if I have to."

She nodded.

I leaned forward and shoved out into the creek. I made wide breaststrokes, trying to envision keeping myself perpendicular to the bank. But everything was black and disorienting. I couldn't see in front of me. My eyes were useless and only confusing me. I closed them and felt the wind gust against my cheek and remembered from what direction it had come and tried to keep swimming so that I continued to feel it there. Francie's hands were cold and tight and trembling against my throat. I heard Liza beside me.

When I felt the tug of current it was heavy and slow, and I knew we were somewhere in the middle of the creek. I kept on, envisioning where we might come out. There was a crooked cypress that Dad usually used as a landmark for the trail, but I didn't expect to find it. Even if we missed the usual route in, I was confident I could still locate the mounds.

When my arms swept over a thatch of palmetto I knew we were across. The swim had been smooth and easy. I grabbed a tree and swung my feet toward the ground. I hefted Francie onto my shoulders, then turned and helped Liza stand.

"You okay?" I asked her.

"Yes," she said.

The floodwater was up to my chest and nearly to Liza's neck. It was really getting to us now, bringing down our body temperatures. I was shivering and I heard Liza's teeth chattering. I had to hold the light over my head with one arm and Francie with the other. She rocked on my shoulders as I made slow and deliberate progress toward the mounds. My feet and legs were constantly tangled in something. It helped to lean against the trees and steady myself, but sometimes there was nothing and I stepped into depressions and stumbled forward, dumping Francie into the cold water. Normally she was a good swimmer for a six-year-old, but her strength and motivation were sapped.

With none of the usual trails and landmarks it was hard to know just how much farther we had to go, and if we were even headed in the right direction. Soon, though, a wailing sound pierced the wind and rain and raised the hair on the back of my neck. Whatever it was, it was directly in front of us. Right where I figured the mounds to be.

25

IT WAS A HORRIBLE, NONHUMAN SCREAM. I STOPPED and studied the weave of tree branches, whipping and slashing before my face.

"What was it?" Liza said through chattering teeth.

"I don't know," I said.

"It came from ahead of us."

"I know," I said.

We had to get out of the water. Even if it didn't rise another inch, we were all close to hypothermic. I started forward again. We hadn't gone far when I heard another wail, followed by an explosion against the surface like a herd of cattle stampeding across a river. I felt fear rise hot up my back, but I didn't stop this time. I didn't want to talk to Liza about it. I didn't know what it was, but it didn't matter. We had to reach the mounds.

I felt the ground slope up beneath my feet. I continued forward until I was standing only waist-deep in the water. Liza came up behind me.

"This is one of the smaller mounds," I said. "The big one we need to get to is a little farther."

"What's making all the noise, Cort?"

"I don't know," I said.

"How much farther?"

"Maybe seventy yards."

I pointed my light in the general direction, and through the rain I saw the reflective eyes of another animal on the mound just ahead of us. I kept my light on it, slowly making out the shape of a buck, standing up to his neck in the floodwater. He stared at us helplessly, numbed and fearless. Then the horror of what we were about to find hit me.

The animals of the swamp were all going for the mounds. No different from us, they knew it was their only refuge for miles. *But why is this buck hanging back?* I wondered. I was pretty sure I knew—still, I didn't want to think about it. And again it didn't matter. We had no choice.

I stepped down into the deep water again and pressed forward. We passed within ten feet of the buck while he stood there, strangely paralyzed. Gradually I saw other animals standing on the low mounds around us. All of the small rises held a deer or a hog, still as statues. I tried to keep the light focused ahead, but it was hard not to

111

turn it on the various grunts and squeals and splashing and scratching of things clawing their way up into the trees. Then there was another explosion of stampeding animals from directly ahead, and I saw the vague white froth of the disturbance and felt the water as it slapped cold against us.

"Crap," I said aloud.

I hadn't meant to say it. I felt Liza come up against me and grab the waist of my pants. Francie trembled on my shoulders and I tightened my grip on her arm. I pulled and carried them along through this eerie isle of prisoners, feeling panic begin to rise within me, moving helplessly toward whatever lay ahead.

Something large and black, grunting and woofing, paddled past us. I stopped and put my light on its face. The bear cocked its eyes at us but kept on. The sight was too much for Francie. She screamed, letting out everything she'd been holding in. The scream flared the panic into my chest as I imagined everything alerted to our approach.

"It's okay," Liza said. "It's just a black bear. It won't hurt us."

But Francie was frantic. She hugged my head and squeezed her hands around my throat. I put the light in my mouth again and lifted my other hand from the water to hold her. Liza came past and pulled me forward.

"Just keep on," she said.

The squealing noise pierced the storm again, followed by the splashing and grunts of animals in chaos. Francie continued to scream and clutch my head. I heaved forward to close the distance to the big mound.

I heard more thrashing and grunting just to my left, and I swung the light and saw two alligators twisting and tearing at a hog carcass. A ringing sound filled my ears, and it felt like I was running through syrup.

"Go!" I said. "Go!"

26

THE MOUND WAS A HILL OF TERROR-STRICKEN hogs and deer and other, smaller animals.

I waved my light. "Hoa!" I yelled.

They parted and scattered before us as we scrambled up the incline.

I continued to wave the light and yell. "Hoa!"

There were eyes everywhere. Things crashed off and scratched their way up trees on all sides. I hefted Francie under my arm, and we slipped and scraped our way up the leafy wetness.

I had rightly guessed that the storm surge would never get high enough to cover the big mound, but we had an entirely different set of problems to deal with now. To the alligators we were no different from the pigs and the deer. The only thing we had going for us was that there were so many other animals to choose from. While the alligators could certainly come onto the land anytime they chose, I reasoned they'd stay in the shallows, where they had the lazy ease of drowning their prey. But as the water rose, they were going to rise with it. Getting out of the water wasn't going to be good enough. We had to get off the ground, too.

There were several trees growing on the mound, but none as large as the juniper at the top. And I hoped the branches were low enough that we could climb it. But there was no end to the dangers in this place. I knew any animals that could climb had the same idea.

Liza had stopped. I crawled up beside her and gave her Francie. Then I took the light from my mouth and waved it around us. The deer had already scattered into the underbrush, but the hogs were bolder. Several small black ones hesitated before backing away. A giant rust-colored boar with six-inch yellow tusks stood his ground, fearless of the light.

This is our ground, he seemed to say.

I looked uphill and saw the trunk of the juniper and grabbed Liza's arm.

"We're getting up in a tree over there," I told her.

Liza followed my gaze.

"As this water comes up those pigs and alligators are coming up with it."

She nodded that she understood. "This could go on for days, Cort," she said.

"We'll do what we have to do."

"Nobody knows we're out here."

"Don't think about that. We'll think about getting back later."

Another pig squealed and thrashed from somewhere below us. I pulled Francie from her. "Come on, Liza," I said. "This is the last thing we have to do tonight."

I stood with Francie and waved the light and yelled to keep the pigs back. We came to the juniper, and I set Francie down and shined the light up into it. The lowest branch was within reach. Liza suddenly yelped and I pulled the light away in time to see the rust-colored hog brush past her, knocking her into the leaves. I yelled at the beast and watched it stop and turn to us only feet away. Fearless. Nowhere else to go. Two more smaller hogs closed in behind it. I helped Liza to her feet and pulled her to the tree trunk.

"Go," I said. "I'll help you up and give Francie to you."

She reached for the low limb and I grabbed her waist and shoved her. In a moment she was crouched above me, reaching down. I passed Francie to her, and then both of them were standing, hugging the trunk.

"Keep going," I said to Liza. "As high as you can. I'm right behind you."

A sharp pain sliced across my leg and something bulky

and hairy knocked me against the tree. I knew instantly I'd been tusked by Rusty, but I didn't have time to worry about it. I got to my feet again, reached for the low branch, and pulled myself up after the girls. The hogs closed in beneath us, blocking our escape.

27

I FOUND THE GIRLS ABOUT TEN FEET UP, FRANCIE hugging the trunk and Liza facing her, holding on above her head. As big and stout as the tree was, it swayed and creaked against the wind. I came up the opposite side from them, my leg throbbing with pain. I put the light on it and saw a three-inch tear in my thigh. Blood ran down my leg, thin and pink and watered down like cherry Kool-Aid.

"Cort!" Liza exclaimed.

"I'll be okay."

"It's gonna get infected."

She was right. I imagined it was already crawling with all the invisible bacteria from the yellow pig tusk.

"I'll worry about it later," I said. "I have to get you two comfortable."

I shined my light about. And then I flashed on something I hadn't expected. Through the branches I caught sight of the black bear we'd seen earlier, clinging to a tree next to us. I studied it for a moment until it slowly turned its head and stared at me.

"He climbed a tree, too," Francie said.

I hadn't meant for her to see it, but for some reason the bear didn't frighten her this time. I pulled the light away.

"Yeah," I said. "Mr. Bear's got a treehouse just like us," I said.

"We can't do this, Cort," Liza said.

I put my light on them. Their legs trembled with fatigue and their teeth chattered. Perched like we were, it wouldn't be long before we collapsed and tumbled into the hogs below.

"We have to," I said. "Just hang on for a little longer. Keep the ants off her."

I snapped branches and placed them at my feet, using the limb I was standing on and another just around the trunk as supports. It didn't take long to construct a rough bench. Then I took off my life vest and spread it for a cushion. In a moment I had Liza on the bench with Francie pulled close for warmth. The ends of the branches were still thick with juniper needles and berries.

"Mr. Bear doesn't have anything to sit on," Francie said.

"Mr. Bear is good at climbing trees," I said. "He's real comfortable."

"He can't get over here, can he?" Liza asked.

"No," I said. "We're fine. Start picking the berries. Chew 'em into a paste and rub it over yourselves. It'll help with the ants. And give Francie a few to eat. She won't like 'em, but chew it up for her and make her swallow."

Liza nodded.

If it were any other girl but Liza with me, we'd be dead, I thought.

I left them and moved about the tree with the light in my mouth, collecting more branches and returning with them to build out the platform. At one point I felt something sticky and abrasive on my wrist and held it before the light to see a cottonmouth transferring from the branch to my arm. I slung it off me and froze, breathing hard, fear humming in my ears.

It was like I could hear Dad talking. *Snakes are just cold and evil. You can't breed it out of them. It's like reptiles got a different God.*

I saw more of them, mostly draped on the ends of the branches, black and thick.

We have to get rid of the snakes first, I thought. *That's more urgent than finishing the platform.*

I found a branch that I could make into a pole about the size of a broomstick. I wash-boarded the pole against the bark of the juniper until I had the knot spikes worn smooth. Then I returned to the girls, huddled wordlessly on the stick platform. Juniper needles and leaves clung to their skin.

There was not enough room for me to sit, so I crouched beside them and leaned against the trunk for support.

"You want to switch for a while?" Liza asked me.

I shook my head.

She continued to slowly chew the berry-like juniper cones.

"Did you give Francie some?" I asked.

Liza nodded.

"Keeping chewing 'em," I said. "Start rubbing it on your skin. It should help with the ants."

"I've never heard of it."

"I think I have. It won't hurt to try."

"What about your leg?" she said.

"It's fine. We'll put some on there, too."

She removed a bit of the paste from her mouth and pressed it tenderly into the wound. It burned, and I hoped that was a sign that it had some antiseptic qualities. When she was done I put the light in my mouth and smashed the compass against the tree. I kept the broken pieces in my fist and removed the largest of the glass shards. Then I began the tedious process of sharpening the pole.

I quickly found that my hands were shaking too much and the glass shard was too small for me to get a purchase on. I located a split in one of the platform branches and pressed the glass into it, making something like a planer to draw the pole against.

The rain wasn't letting up. The only reprieve we had was when a gust of wind came against the backside of the trunk and blew the water around us. The hogs continued to squeal and grunt below. I counted five of the smaller black ones, plus Rusty, packed against the base of the tree. I didn't see any deer, and assumed they were hidden somewhere in the underbrush beyond. It was still too dark to see far without the light, but I heard what must have been more of the beasts arriving at the base of the mound.

"Dad," I said.

"What?" Liza said.

I realized I was talking to myself and shook my head. "Nothing."

But I thought about him. In a strange way I sensed he was with me, telling me what to do, guiding my hands. I realized I was no more than the things he'd taught me. *But why had he left me to face this alone? Where was he when I needed him most?* I'd never felt so abandoned.

28

I CROUCHED AND HUDDLED AGAINST THE GIRLS TO try and keep them warm while the weather beat at my bare back. After a while I became numb to it, like something in a hard shell. I held them and it felt good not to have to think or do anything for a change.

It wasn't until Francie mentioned stars that I noticed the rain no longer pelted me and the wind was no longer howling through the treetops. I lifted my head and saw the canopy was still and the swamp wasn't as dark.

"She's right," Liza said. "Stars."

I looked up through the limbs and saw the night speckled with pinpoints of light, as cloudless as the clearest sky I'd ever seen.

"The storm's gone," Liza said.

"For now," I said. I wasn't sure if she was trying to give Francie hope or if she didn't really know what was happening. "We're in the eye of the hurricane. Right in the middle."

"So—" Liza didn't finish her sentence.

"That's right," I said. I reached out and brushed Francie's hair from her face and pressed my palm against her cheek. The skin was cold. Her lips were starting to get a bluish color to them.

"Can we get down now, Cort?" Francie whispered.

"Not yet, Francie," I said. "Y'all need to drink water."

I leaned forward and bit into Liza's flotation vest and tore the fabric. Once the tear was started I ripped around the foam panel until I had a rectangular piece of watertight cloth. I held it against the tree and caught water as it drained down the trunk. When I had a small bowlful I cupped it and made a spout and held it to her face.

"Open your mouth," I said.

She did. Water trickled down the cup and she swallowed as it ran over her tongue. I waited until she closed her lips and it rolled off her chin. Then I bent down and tilted Francie's head and did the same for her.

When they'd both had enough, I drank a little myself. Then I pressed the fabric into Liza's hands and told her to hold on to it.

I could think of nothing else to do for us. The bear moaned and I put my light on him and saw him clutching the tree, trembling. I couldn't tell if he was cold, tired, or sick.

The hogs grunted below. I didn't want the girls thinking about any of it. I wanted them to keep talking. To keep their minds on something else. Liza must have been thinking the same thing.

"I'll bet Mr. Bear has a name," she said.

"I'll bet he does," I said. "What do you think his name is, Francie?"

"Elmo," she mumbled.

Liza and I laughed.

"Elmo," Liza repeated. "I think you're right. Another Elmo."

"Elmo needs water, too," Francie mumbled.

"I don't know how we can get water to him," Liza said, "but Elmo's used to getting water out here in the swamp. I think he knows what to do."

"What about the snakes?" Francie said.

"I don't see any snakes over there," I said.

"You have to look," she said.

"Okay," I said. "I'll look. I'll make sure Elmo doesn't have any snakes in the tree with him."

I stood with my spear. The bear was about ten feet away and my stick was only six feet long. I knew there would be snakes in that tree, and I didn't know what I could do about it. But I wanted to convince Francie I'd done something.

I put the light in my mouth and grabbed a branch overhead. I used it for balance as I slowly made my way out on one of the limbs supporting our platform. The bear turned its head and watched me.

The limb bowed under my weight. "Coming toward you, Elmo," I said nervously.

When I'd gone as far as I could, I moved my head about, shining the bear's tree. I saw two snakes coiled directly below him, the pearl black of their eyes blinkless and cruel. I held the stick out toward him, and he grunted and shifted.

"Easy, Elmo," I said.

I used the tip of the spear to flick the two snakes off the limb. As I was doing so, I saw another just out of reach. I'd done what I could, so I backed up until I was on firmer footing again. The bear kept his eyes on me. Closer now, I saw something yellow dripping from the edge of his mouth. He was sick. I guessed he'd already been snakebit.

"Hang in there, Elmo," I said.

While I was out on the limb with a different viewpoint, I made a quick scan of our own tree. I saw a larger snake above us and out of reach. But I didn't say anything. Maybe it was best if the girls didn't suspect what I was starting to realize. There were snakes everywhere. And they were going to keep coming.

29

WHEN I RETURNED TO THE GIRLS I SAW THEIR SKIN was covered with thin smears of chewed juniper berries. Liza had been applying more of the paste while I was out on the limb. The wind and rain was starting up again and the swamp was growing darker.

"The stars are gone," Liza said.

I didn't need to look up to see that the eye of the hurricane had passed and the storm clouds were moving back over us. And I knew the second act of Igor, the messy trailing end of him, was going to be even wetter than the first.

"How much longer before daylight?" I said.

She pulled her hand from her lap and looked at her watch. "It's four o'clock," she said.

"Two hours," I said.

She looked back at me, as if waiting for some solution I'd thought of.

"Two more hours, and Dad'll come home and start searching for us."

She continued to look at me. She didn't say anything, but her eyes told me what she was thinking. I didn't need to make up anything with her. She knew better.

"Will the storm get worse?"

"The wind'll change directions. It should start blowing some of this water out of here."

Liza shifted and drew up her knee. Suddenly she yelped and kicked outward. I waved the light over her leg and saw a cottonmouth hanging and whipping from her heel. Francie screamed and twisted against her. I leaned against the trunk and swiped at it with the spear. Liza was kicking wildly and I missed twice before I was able to connect with enough of the snake's body to tear it loose. She pulled her leg back under her and gripped her heel tightly, her chest rising and falling in deep breaths of panic. Francie was hysterical again, and Liza instinctively pulled her to her.

"Dammit," I said, trying to hold myself together. "Dammit. Hold on." I knelt and fumbled for the glass shard. "Hold on," I said again.

I brushed my hand over it and felt the glass slice into my palm. I winced and found it again and pulled it from the split. I sat and hung my legs on the outside of the platform and reached for her foot.

"Let go of it," I said.

"I'm in trouble now," she said.

She rocked and moaned and held it and didn't seem to hear me.

"Liza!"

She let go and I put the light on her heel and saw the two fang marks, oozing something milky and bloody. I held her ankle tight and sliced quickly from one puncture to the other. She yelped and jerked, and I pulled the heel back to me. Then I leaned over and sucked and spit the poison.

Liza managed to calm herself for Francie. "Shhh," she said to her. "It's gonna be okay. Look, Cort's fixing it."

But I felt her leg trembling and I knew she didn't believe what she was saying. I didn't want to think about whether I believed it or not.

Francie stopped wailing and hugged her tightly.

"Did you get it all?" Liza said. She asked me in a way that didn't sound like she really cared about the answer.

There was no way to get it all, but she didn't need the truth. "I tasted it," I said. "I got a lot of it."

"What's gonna happen to me?"

"I don't know."

"Yes, you do, Cort. You know about this."

She was right. I did. But I wished I didn't.

30

I'D SEEN A MAN SNAKEBIT BEFORE. A PASTY-skinned bird-watcher from Minnesota, a retired attorney we took on a day trip. He was chasing a blue heron we'd seen flap and croak away. Dad was always impatient with bird-watchers, but more so with this man than usual. He'd ignored everything we'd said that day regarding his safety. Dad told him there would be other herons and not to get out of the boat. But he didn't listen. He held his eyeglasses with one hand and clutched his camera with the other and left the boat sweating and thrashing into a steamy thicket.

We stayed behind and drank some water and waited. A moment later we heard him deep in the underbrush, screaming like a girl.

"He's prob'ly up to his waist in mud," Dad said to me. "Got a big banana spider on his face."

I smiled. Dad and I often joked about banana spiders. They were an evil black-and-yellow color and grew as big as my hand. They always seemed to string their webs right where a person wanted to walk, sometimes two or more clinging to the same web. Although they weren't poisonous, that didn't help matters when you passed through a sticky mess of them and felt them crawling over your neck and face.

"You want me to go help him?" I asked.

Dad frowned and started to stand. He sighed. "Naw, I'll check on him."

Dad took his time capping the thermos and replacing it in the cooler. Before he was done we heard the attorney crashing toward us through the palmetto. He reappeared at the water's edge, his glasses gone, bright red streaks of briar tears across his face. He held his arm and stared at us with a look of horror.

"I've been bitten by a viper," he said in disbelief.

I looked at Dad. He didn't seem immediately alarmed. The man had been overreacting to things all day. We helped him into the boat and he showed us the two fang marks on the muscle of his forearm.

"What did the snake look like?" Dad asked him.

"It was black and thick."

"Are you sure it was venomous?"

"What?" the birder said. "I don't know anything about vipers!"

"Was its head thick and triangular?"

"I didn't study its head, you idiot! Let's go! I need medical attention!"

I was already starting our old tiller-steer jon. Snakebite or not, I knew Dad was ready to get the birder back to the landing.

"Calm down," Dad told him. "If it was venomous, then you need to keep your heart rate slow."

"Go, kid!" the birder screamed.

The boat was backing off the bank. I couldn't have gone any faster. Dad got the snakebite kit out of a dry box under his seat. He pulled it open and dumped the contents into his lap. Meanwhile I gunned the boat up the bayou.

"What's that?" the birder asked.

"Snakebite kit. There's a razor blade in here. We'll need to cut your arm and start sucking out the venom."

"Cut me! What if it's not poisonous?"

"It probably was," Dad said to him.

He studied us for a moment as if there were a possibility Dad was joking. I held the tiller of the boat as we raced up the bayou. We had a twenty-minute ride ahead of us to the landing. If he'd been bitten by a cottonmouth, then it was more important to get him to a hospital than it was to suck the venom. There were even some people we knew who discouraged using a snakebite kit at all if there was a chance of proper medical attention. But I knew what Dad was thinking. Maybe just keeping the guy occupied would calm him down.

"Hold out your arm," Dad said.

"Do you have any experience with this?" the birder said.

"No."

"I want certified medical attention!"

"Suit yourself," Dad said.

Dad put away the snakebite kit and got our two-way radio from a dry bag at my feet and called Curly Stanson, the sheriff.

"Curly, I've got a client that may have been bitten by a cottonmouth. You think you could get somebody to meet me? I'm about fifteen minutes out."

"Ten-four," Curly said. "I'll get 'em on the way."

"Who was that?" the lawyer said.

"The sheriff."

"Call an ambulance or something! I don't know where the hospital is! What do you expect *him* to do?"

"There's no cell phone coverage here. He'll have somebody drive you to the hospital."

"What kind of jackleg outfit is this?"

Dad looked him straight in the eyes. "Do you want to die?"

"What the hell kind of question is that?"

"There's snake venom in your bloodstream. Possibly enough to kill you. The more you move, the more you talk, the faster your heart pumps it through your entire body. It's already eatin' at the muscle tissue in your arm. If you're lucky, they won't have to amputate it."

The birder swallowed and didn't answer.

"So turn around, face forward, and shut up."

The birder nodded like a child and slowly turned in his seat. I didn't hear him speak again. We got him to the landing, where Curly himself was waiting to take him away. After they left Dad told me he'd probably try to sue us. He never did, but the doctor had to cut off the birder's arm at the elbow.

31

I WIPED THE RAINWATER FROM MY FACE AND SPAT.

"It won't kill you," I told Liza. "But it's gonna get swollen. You'll feel sick."

"Check the tree, Cort. Make sure there aren't more."

Of course there were more. But I pulled myself up again and passed the light along the limb beneath my feet. I saw a smaller one, but the immature ones were the worst. They typically overinjected venom. I used the end of my spear to gently dislodge it so that it fell onto the backs of the pigs below.

"It's just a little one," I said.

She didn't answer me. I continued the search, contorting myself into every possible position to see around the trunk and beneath the platform. I found another and flicked it into the air. I studied every inch of the bark until I saw the black reflections of their eyes. I removed five in just the areas I was able to search with the weak light. I knew there were more. I knew more were coming.

Liza and Francie suffered quietly beside me, balled up,

shivering, water running down their faces. I didn't want to see Liza's foot in the darkness. I tried not to think about any of it. The most I could do was try to keep things from getting worse. If Francie took one bite like that, it would kill her. If Liza took another, she didn't stand a chance either.

I tried to act brave for the girls, tried to make them believe I knew what I was doing, but inside my head I was a mess.

Dad, I thought. *What do I do, Dad?*

I tried not to be angry at him. In a strange way, I thought if I was angry then he wouldn't help me. I spent the final two hours of darkness on my stomach, watching the trunk below, occasionally glimpsing Rusty or one of the smaller hogs. The juniper rocked slowly against the storm. I looked over at the bear. He was trying to climb higher, but he was making a weak effort of it. I felt a connection to the beast in his own private battle. I looked away and thought again about the difference between mammals and reptiles.

Pigs can make gentle pets when raised in captivity. And, of course, so can dogs. I've even seen pet bears on television. With mammals, if you take away their need to constantly search for food, it seems to make room in their heads for love and loyalty and companionship. But make them fend for themselves, and they turn into killers. A dog turns into a wolf. A pig grows coarse hair and tusks and slims down into a lethal thug.

I studied the bear again, still struggling to climb. I wondered if friendly feelings were buried deep in his thick head. Feelings that hadn't been completely extinguished by the daily struggle of survival.

I worried that there were snakes above us. I didn't know why there wouldn't be. The bear could be climbing toward them.

Stay still. Don't move like that. Daylight will be here soon.

Any snakes above us would most likely stay where they were or go higher. It was certain death for them to leave the trees. The best I could do was stop the flow of them up into our space. Keep them off the girls. I gripped the spear tightly and resumed my watch.

The swamp slowly revealed itself in dull, diluted light. Through the rain I made out not just the backs of the hogs but their eyes and their tusks as well. Two deer standing in the brush. The green of leaves and yellow of cane stems. Everything wet and pressed. There were no birdcalls, no squirrel chatter. Only the soft grunting of the pigs and an occasional thrashing in the water downhill. With the onset of morning a relative calmness had settled over the mound.

I worked my way into a sitting position and turned to the girls. My eyes went straight to Liza's foot. It was swollen to twice its size, purple and black with streaks of red running up her ankle. Both of them were shivering with cold and sickness, their heads buried into each other, Francie balled tightly into her lap.

"Liza," I said.

She didn't answer me.

"It's morning."

She shifted slightly and grew still again. I wanted her to talk to me.

"Liza, do you remember when we used catch the bullfrogs in the creek? We brought them to Dad, and he cleaned them and fried the legs for us. We had fried frog legs. Remember that?"

She didn't move.

"They were so small it was like eating crab claws. But we thought it was the best thing in the world."

The wind gusted and a wet leaf slapped against her cheek. I reached out and pulled it away.

"Liza? Remember? We were gonna go into business together and make a lot of money selling frog legs."

Nothing.

"Liza? Just say something to me."

"I feel sick," she muttered.

"Okay," I said. "Don't say anything, then. Just stay still."

I studied her foot again. I thought about cutting slices in it to relieve the pressure. Then I thought about the open wounds getting infected. As with the rest of our situation, there seemed to be no clear choices. Then I felt my own wound throbbing on my leg and looked down to see the nasty tear, rain-washed and hanging open like a cut of raw steak. The same red streaks of infection ran up my thigh.

Just how many ways can there be to die in this place? I wondered.

32

I REACHED OUT AND PICKED SOME JUNIPER BERRIES and chewed them into the sappy paste. I pressed some gently against the slice I'd made across Liza's fang marks. She jerked slightly but didn't complain.

If we live she might lose her leg. And it will change her. But it won't change the way I feel about her. She's the bravest person I'll ever know.

I picked more of the berries and chewed them. I looked into the treetops and studied the swamp canopy. It wasn't whipping and thrashing as it had during the night. Occasionally a quick gust rocked the juniper and sprayed us with leaves and wet cold. The sky was a rain-drizzling blanket of dirty cotton. Igor wasn't done with us, but it was weakening. I imagined we were now beneath a wide expanse of tropical storm the hurricane collected and dragged in its wake.

I applied the juniper paste to the gash on my leg, trying to ignore the dull pain of it. Then I studied the scene below. I couldn't see the edge of the floodwater through the tangle of tree limbs, but I knew it could only be forty or fifty feet downhill.

Suddenly Rusty squealed from somewhere to my left and I heard the smaller pigs crash away into the under-brush. I turned to see him stomping and ripping the dirt with his tusks. In a moment he backed away with a snake in his mouth, shook it several times, and slung it. The lifeless body slapped limp and wet against a tree trunk. Rusty grunted and pawed the dirt again. Then he made a sideways dash and repeated the routine on another snake.

As Rusty continued to find and kill snakes, the small black pigs reappeared. One of them went over to a dead cottonmouth and sniffed it. Then it began tearing it apart and eating it.

Liza moaned something and I turned back to the girls.

"It's just the pigs," I said. "They can't get up here. Francie, what do you want for Christmas this year?"

She didn't raise her head, but she answered me. "A fire truck," she mumbled.

"A fire truck?"

She moved her chin against Liza's shoulder. "A real one," she said. "So Catfish can ride in it."

I smiled.

"Liza, do you remember when we watched that movie

about the people that went to the center of the earth? Remember, we got the shovels and started digging a hole in your backyard?

She didn't respond.

"You don't have to answer," I said. "I'll talk and both of you can listen. We did that, Francie. We thought we could dig a hole to another place where there would be dinosaurs and underground lakes. It got to be a pretty big hole. Then it rained and filled—"

Something slammed into the tree below. It sounded like a person hit it with a baseball bat. I looked down to see Rusty backing away. Blood ran down his mouth, and his body trembled and shook in a crazed, rabid way. Francie began to whimper softly.

"He can't get up here," I reassured her. "It's all right."

Rusty pawed the dirt and charged again, throwing his body against the juniper like he wanted to knock us out of it. The tree didn't shake much, but I found myself gripping the limbs tightly. Rusty ran at the tree again, this time hitting it with his tusks. Then he swung his face against the bark and dug his cutter teeth into it, sawing them back and forth, shredding long white gashes into the trunk.

He's gone insane.

I reasoned he'd been snakebit, but I'd never seen an animal acting so enraged.

The hog spent several minutes sawing at the juniper until he suddenly spun and charged the bear's tree. He hit and attacked it with the same force. The bear groaned and I looked over at him. He had his face tucked down so that I couldn't see his eyes, but I saw his stomach rising and falling. The groan seemed to enrage Rusty more. He circled the water oak, waving his head up and down, shredding the bark.

After a few minutes Rusty stopped attacking the trees. The other pigs were picking through the leaves, finding dead and live snakes and eating them. Rusty suddenly charged one of them and toppled it into the underbrush. What followed was a deafening blend of squeals over a blur of brown and black hair. The other pigs scattered away in terror. Soon the bushes were still and Rusty appeared, his tusks dripping with blood. He studied the juniper for a second, then turned and charged into the underbrush again. For several minutes there was more squealing and thrashing. Something crashed into the water. Then a few soft grunts. Then silence.

He wants us to think he's gone.

I grabbed a stick and dropped it. The second it hit the ground Rusty came charging from the underbrush and stomped it to splinters. Though I knew he couldn't get to us, his determination convinced me at last that the mound was going to kill us one way or another unless I did something about it. Staying in the tree was as good as giving up.

"I'm going for help," I said.

Liza didn't look at me, but she reached over and put her hand on my arm and squeezed gently.

"I have to get both of you out of here."

She lifted her head slightly and turned to me and opened her eyes.

"Can you hang on for a while longer?" I asked.

"I feel sick," she said.

"I know. Drink more water whenever you can. Don't lose that fabric."

"I'm afraid I'm gonna drop Francie."

Liza had three parallel straps securing her flotation vest. I unclipped the top one and tugged it. She moved slightly to allow it to pass through the loops on the back side. I got it free and pulled the clips to the extreme ends of the strap. I saw it wasn't going to be long enough, so I took another one and tied the ends together.

"I'm gonna strap both of you to the tree," I said.

She squeezed my arm again. "What can you do?"

"I don't know. I have to try something. I can't just sit here."

I ran the strap around the trunk and passed it beneath the shoulder of Francie's vest and then fully around Liza.

I clipped the two ends together and cinched it snug. Then I got the spear and placed it before Liza.

"The pigs are killing the snakes," I said. "I don't think any more will be coming up the tree . . . But take this in case."

"There's nobody out there, Cort."

"I know. And there's nobody coming. And this flood-water isn't gonna back off any time soon."

"But the alligators."

I glanced at Francie, then back at Liza, and I saw in her eyes that she knew what I didn't want to say.

"We don't have much time," I said.

She started to reach for the life vest beneath them and I grabbed her arm and stopped her.

"It'll just slow me," I said. "I've thought about it."

She pulled her hand into her lap again. She began to cry softly.

33

RUSTY PANTED AND PACED IN A CIRCLE BELOW. I didn't see the smaller hogs. I reasoned he'd killed at least two. If there were survivors, they were probably hiding in the underbrush.

Even if I figured out some way to get past Rusty to the water, I'd still have the alligators to contend with. But we had made it past them the first time. I just had to do it again. Through more.

I looked out into the canopy. I wondered if it was possible to leap through the trees until I was past Rusty and out over the water. But the only trees close enough to jump to didn't look like they'd hold my weight—except for the large water oak the bear was in. From there the ground began to slope down and I saw some other saplings that might hold me.

Crazy. The bear looked like he had the same sickness as Rusty. *He could tear me to pieces.*

But I *knew* Rusty wouldn't hesitate to attack. I wasn't

so sure about the bear. Even if he was as crazy as the hog, he wasn't in an ideal position to attack anything.

If I could jump out and grab the tree below him . . . Maybe I'll have time to jump again before he can get at me.

My heart beat faster as I fully comprehended what I was setting myself up for. I fought back my fear and tried to reason with myself.

There's no other way. Not unless you can outrun Rusty . . . Which you can't.

There was no safer option.

I got the spear from Liza and walked out on the limb. The bear turned his head and looked at me. I held the pole out slowly and saw his eyes follow the end of it. I gently nudged him on his haunch.

"Come on, big fellow," I said.

The bear shifted slightly and growled with irritation.

"Don't hurt Elmo," Francie mumbled.

"I'm not," I said.

I poked the bear again and he shuffled a few inches up the tree.

"There you go," I said.

I gave him another poke and he continued another five or six feet and out of my reach. I wished he were higher, but that was all I was going to get.

I returned to Liza and placed the spear in her lap again.

"Cort?" she muttered.

"It's fine," I said. "I've got to go. There's no other way."

She lifted her head and looked at me. Her eyes were still red and wet. "Is Francie gonna fall?"

"No, I've got her strapped in good. She's not gonna fall. Neither one of you are."

She nodded and lowered her head again. I brushed the hair out of Francie's face and checked the straps again, making sure they were tight. Then I stood and walked back out on the limb.

I studied what I was about to do. After a minute I saw there was no good way to go about it. I just had to jump and start grabbing for a handhold. Then get to another tree as fast as I could.

I leaped out and crashed into the limbs of the bear's tree, flailing my arms for a handhold, images of snakes and Rusty flashing through my head like a nightmare. In the midst of it all I heard Elmo roar like he was right at my ear. Everything was fast and blurry and confusing.

I caught a weak limb six feet below where I'd jumped. I heard Rusty going mad beneath me, tearing at the water oak. I quickly looked up and saw the bear looking down at me. He hadn't moved.

I clawed my way to the tree and hugged it, trying to smother the paralyzing fear racing through me. I heard the bear moving and felt the tree rocking. When I looked up again he was climbing higher.

Yes, just what I needed. Time to think.

Even with Rusty enraged below, I had to calm myself and get my thoughts together. The water was still out of sight. But as the hill descended, so did the tops of the trees. I thought it might be possible to jump into the upper branches of another water oak at least once more. I stabilized my feet and judged my options. I soon found another small tree and leaped out, into the thick of it.

When I was secure against the second tree, I looked down to see Rusty still stalking me. Suddenly a doe crashed away through the underbrush. Then I saw a nutria, a giant rat the size of a beaver, scamper under a log. There were still other animals alive on the mound. Rusty hadn't killed them all. I looked out through the weave of leaves and sticks to where I glimpsed the reflection of water. It was the color of chocolate milk, undulating and wavy. But there were no more large trees to leap into. I'd gone as far as I could go.

I was still high in the tree and decided to get below the leaves to fully assess my options again. I started down, watching my feet as I felt for branches, looking for snakes. As I dropped closer to the ground I saw the three remaining hogs uphill of my position. Rusty stepped closer and snorted and watched me. About eight feet from the ground

I was able to better study the water. None of the animals were standing near it. Even Rusty seemed hesitant to come farther downhill. And then I saw why.

Four alligators lay black and still at the water's edge. They were impervious to the wind and rain. They had nothing better to do than float there and wait patiently. About them were the torn pink rain-washed carcasses of partly eaten animals. Mostly hogs, a few deer, and snakes. Beyond them were several other alligators. I'd never seen so many in one place. And there was no telling how many more were on the other sides of the mound. Everything, including me, was going to have to get past their cold eyes and teeth sooner or later.

34

I CLUNG TO THE TREE, DELAYING WHAT I KNEW was probably a leap to my death. Rusty snorted again and rubbed his face in the dirt.

Get it over with, I thought.

I returned my attention to the few remaining trees downhill. There were no more within reach that would support my weight. The only option I saw was a thin hackberry. I reasoned if I could leap to its trunk it might bend with me toward the water's edge. Perhaps enough to drop me over the alligators on the bank. Then I would have to swim for my life. I was fast in the water, but Rusty and the alligators were certainly faster.

I need a better plan.

"Dad," I said aloud.

But no one was there. It seemed pointless to even make a plan. There was no good plan.

The situation is impossible. I am going to meet the same agonizing death as the rest of the carcasses in the water.

So I thought of pain instead, to brace myself for death.

Dad told me once that animals gripped in the jaws of predators didn't feel pain. That a body overloaded with instant deep-tissue damage was numb. But the thought was no comfort. I looked back toward the girls. I couldn't see them. Then I felt crushing loneliness and I wanted to be back with Liza. I didn't want to die alone.

Think. What are your options? You can't hang on to this tree for long. And you can't go back. There's only one choice.

"Dad," I said again.

I remembered something else he'd told me. *Don't thrash. Don't excite them. Don't swim like you're scared. Walk if you can.*

I looked at Rusty again. His eyes were locked on me.

He won't get closer to the water. Not while the alligators are there.

I didn't want to think about it anymore. Any of it. I just wanted it over with. I leaped out and crashed into the hackberry. It gave little resistance and bent and snapped, and suddenly I was in the water, sinking in a cold, murky blur. I felt adrenaline rush through me like an electric shock, and I clenched my teeth and fought it away. I put my arms forward and made a wide, controlled stroke to the surface. I broke the water slowly and made an effort not to look until my feet were on the ground. Something rough brushed my leg and swirled the water to my left.

Panic flared white-hot inside me. My muscles locked and I felt my heart drumming like something in a hollow barrel.

"Come on," I muttered. "Hold it together."

I fought back the fear and lowered my feet. I found myself standing in chest-deep water. The ground still sloped beneath me and I realized there wasn't going to be any walking. Everything before me was too deep. In my immediate area I saw no alligators. I was sure they had submerged themselves, startled at the disruption. But I turned and saw the ones behind me, still on the bank, a few of them with their heads up and turned, studying me.

Go, I thought. *Stay calm, and get out of here.*

I leaned forward and pulled my feet up and breast-stroked in the direction of Bottle Creek. Slow, smooth, controlled strokes. Keeping my chin up and eyes ahead of me. Trailing my feet and kicking them as little as possible. I felt something else swirl beneath my stomach. I remained calm. Kept moving.

Something scraped my chest and threatened to send panic screaming through me again. Then I realized it was just a small tree or the top of a palmetto plant.

Keep going.

The noises of the mound faded behind me, and then there was nothing but the rain and the wind in the trees. A cottonmouth passed me on the left, head up, looking not for a fight but a late arrival at the mound. As much as I feared for the girls, I was overwhelmed with relief to be leaving that place.

My fear of the alligators faded and my thoughts turned to my newest problems. I was confident I could swim the mile or so back to the Tensaw, but could I find it? Now I had no compass and everything looked different under floodwater. And if I did find my way back, how would I get across the river?

35

WHEN I ARRIVED AT A GAP IN THE TREES I KNEW
I'd reached Bottle Creek. I hugged a water oak to rest and
look and think. I sensed it was late morning, though it was
hard to know with the sun blotted out behind the thick
cloud cover. The storm gusts were louder as they howled
down the break in the swamp canopy like a canyon wind.

Other than the break in the trees and the ripples on
the surface, there was nothing to distinguish the creek
from the rest of the water. It all flowed like one mass to
the south. I realized that maybe at least one of my problems had a simple solution. Since the entire swamp was
flowing like a river, if I swam perpendicular to the current my course should take me east toward the Tensaw.
Using the wind against my face had worked earlier. Now
I would use the water in the same way. It was rough navigation at best, but even that small clue was enough infor-
mation to encourage me.

I was no longer fearful of the hogs and snakes and
alligators. That was something behind me. Now, water

and time were my real enemies. I had a lot of dangerous water and not enough time. As if prompting me to move on, minnows nibbled at my tusk wound, sending tiny jets of pain up my thigh. I moved my legs again, like waving flies underwater. The swamp wasn't going to allow me even a short rest.

"Hang on, girls," I said aloud.

I pushed out into the creek and kicked my legs and swung my arms against the current. Any other time the swim I faced across a mile of flooded swamp might seem like a death threat in itself, but compared to what I'd been through the night before, it was a vacation. I entered the trees on the other side and passed once again into the shadow of the canopy.

I kept my head up, breaststroking through the strange flooded land. Keeping the current on my cheek, my eyes on the next distant tree ahead, I passed at eye level with squirrels and raccoons and opossums in the treetops. There were more snakes and more ants. I didn't try to avoid them. I had no sense of time, no sense of distance.

Keep your head up. Stroke. Find the tree. Stroke.

I thought about my mother. For the first time in years, I wasn't angry with her. I just wanted her to be okay. I wanted all of us to be okay. The boil of problems between her and Dad seemed like so much time wasted.

I should be glad that she's gone, I thought. *Whatever*

they had just didn't work. She was a girl like Liza once. She didn't see all of this coming. She just wants to be happy. I could like her if she was happy. Dad loves her and he should want that, too. He just doesn't know it. I'd feel the same way if Liza left me. I wouldn't like it, but I'd be happy. For her.

Eventually I arrived at a wide expanse of windblown water. I came up against a cypress tree and hugged it and studied the shape and size of the lake. I soon recognized it as the same one we'd come up against in the night. I kicked away and moved into the trees again to get protection from the wind and rain. I adjusted my course slightly and kept on.

What do women really want? They want a nice house and money and friends. They want men who wear suits and drive new cars. What they don't want is houseboats and smelly men who hunt and fish for a living. Who have dogs named Catfish. I don't want to be this. I won't be this.

I felt the Tensaw before I saw it. A greater pull somewhere out in front of me. A channelized, sucking monster of hydraulic power. I slowed and heard it licking through the trees. The small optimism I'd built left me.

There's no way, I thought. *Dad, there's no way.*

But I kept on, trying to shut out my fear, my reasoning. There was even something peaceful in knowing that soon it would all be over. I'd be swept under and tumbled in the liquid dark, choking for a moment, knowing I'd done what I could before the world went black. Dad once told me that if he had to choose a way to go, it would be drowning. He said there wouldn't be any pain. It made sense to me.

The current overtook my efforts before I reached the river. I stopped swimming and grabbed a tree and held it while my legs trailed downstream. I remained there, the water rushing around the trunk and into my face. The roar of the wind over the river was louder than ever. Like this had always been the source of the storm's violence. I felt my leg muscles begin to spasm. Then the spasms went up into my arms. I pressed my cheek against the rough bark. The girls seemed so far away.

"Dad," I said aloud.

I wanted to get it over with. I was exhausted. I was tired of the game I was playing with myself. *Why do I have to keep trying? What's the point?* And I thought of the girls again and I imagined them strapped helplessly over that death scene.

I can try to suffer more than them. It's the least I can do.

I let go of the tree and allowed the current to suck me backward. I slammed sideways into another tree and felt a sharp pain in my ribs. I twisted and kicked off it. I thrashed from one tree to the next, making slow, diagonal progress toward the giant slurping sound of the river.

Suddenly it was there beside me. The wide roil of it, strewn with white flecks of trash and trees. I clung to a cypress branch, dipping and swinging on the surface.

Find something. A log. Hold on to it. Paddle it. You might not reach the other side for miles, but grab something.

I looked to the far trees, nearly a hundred yards away. Then down and across the surface of the water, the color of creamed coffee, sliding and rolling in upon itself. I watched a stripped tree the size of a telephone pole sucked under in a boil. Moments later it reappeared twenty yards downriver, the nose of it rising like a whale, gaining height, finally overtaken by its own weight, and slapping back to the water again. I knew it wasn't possible to swim across and survive. But my arms and legs were trembling again. The girls were waiting.

Quittin' ain't in my blood, and it ain't in yours.

The white hull of a refrigerator came bobbing toward me, eager and timely. As it passed I leaped out and clawed over it, feeling for a handhold. On the opposite side I found the door splayed open. I crawled partly onto it and wrapped my fingers around the inside edge. Then I kicked my feet beneath the box, trying to propel it across the river. The hydraulics sucked at my legs and spun us. I re-alized that I didn't have the strength to fight anymore. I let my legs relax. I lay my face on the door and tasted the cold, gritty water as it ebbed against my mouth.

"I'm sorry," I said.

36

I DRIFTED DOWNRIVER WITH MY EYES CLOSED, strangely comfortable, no longer worried about anything. The wind and rain beat on my face, and the cold water spun and rocked my limp body amid the storm debris. It seemed there was nothing left of me but a dreamy consciousness keeping my fingers curled around the door, savoring the moment before I let go and sank into the muddy depths.

Then I felt something slam into the refrigerator, almost tearing it from my grip.

"Cort!" someone yelled.

I thought it was just part of the dream.

"Cort!"

I opened my eyes and saw Dad reaching out to hold the edge of the fridge.

"Grab the side of the boat, son!"

Dad hung over me in Mr. Stovall's old center-console jon. When I didn't respond he spun the fridge, leaned out, and grabbed the back of my pants. He pulled me over the gunnels and I flopped to the deck like a big fish.

He leaned down and got in my face. "Where are they?"

I still couldn't make sense of the situation. I began to cough and cry. "Dad."

He punched me hard in the shoulder. "Come on, Cort! Where are they?"

I leaped at him with the last of my strength, hit him on the leg, and fell at his feet. "I hate you," I said. "I hate you."

"I'm here, Cort."

"You were gone!" I coughed. "You left me!"

He grabbed my arm and tried to pull me up. "Come on, son."

I jerked away from him and wiped my face. "It's too late," I said.

For a moment neither of us said anything. The turbulence spun the boat and sucked at it and carried us swiftly downriver. The storm blew and spat at us. But I didn't see or hear or feel any of it. I felt like something curled into a hard shell.

"I'm sorry," he said. "I was wrong to leave. I know that."

"I needed you," I said. "I just need you. It's just us."

He touched my shoulder again. "I know," he said.

After a moment my head began to clear and I said, "The mounds. They're at the mounds."

He pulled his hand away and shoved down on the engine throttle. The boat started swinging against the current.

"Bottle Creek?" he said.

I wiped my face again and grabbed the steering console and started to pull myself up.

"Are they at Bottle Creek?"

"Yes," I said.

I stood and held the running bar of the console. He bent down and grabbed a life vest and shoved it toward me.

"Put it on."

I leaned against the console and worked my arms into the vest while the boat surged upriver, chewing against the current.

"What happened, Cort? I need somethin' to work with here."

I didn't answer his question. "We need guns, Dad."

"What?"

"They're in a tree on top of the big mound. There's a boar hog and alligators and snakes and everything in the swamp. Liza's snakebit. They were both in bad shape when I left them."

Dad bit his bottom lip, trying to get his thoughts around it all.

"We've got to kill the hog, Dad. You can't get past it. It's snakebit or something. It's gone mad."

He swallowed. "The guns are still in my truck," he said. "Way out across Nelson's field."

"We don't have that much time."

He studied the river ahead and didn't answer me.

"Dad!"

He looked at me.

"We can't get past it," I said. "It'll kill us."

He stared ahead again and clenched his jaw with determination. It was a look of resolve I hadn't seen in a long time.

"We'll do what we have to do," he said. "Hang on."

He jammed his palm against the throttle again, hammering all he could get from the outboard. The boat leaped and strained against the river.

37

IT SEEMED TO TAKE FOREVER, PLOWING UPRIVER to the mouth of Bayou Jessamine, wiping water from our faces, dodging debris, and strong-arming the boat through the river boils and undertow.

"We're gonna get those girls, son," Dad shouted over the wind. But the tone of his voice didn't have any confidence behind it. It was just talk to make us both feel better. My eyes searched the boat and my mind raced with ideas, but I could think of nothing we had to fend off Rusty. Dad didn't understand. He hadn't seen what was out there.

Dad pointed at a spot on the west side of the river. I saw the remains of the houseboat, just a few pieces of the roof, twisted and torn and caught up in the trees.

I looked away. "I had to leave Catfish on there," I said. "He wouldn't get off the houseboat."

Dad shook his head like he didn't want to hear any more bad news. After a minute he slammed his hand on the throttle.

"Come on!" he said. "Why can't this thing go faster?"

Finally we swung into the mouth of Bayou Jessamine and had to slow down. The river let go of the boat and the trees closed around, giving us shelter from the storm. The creek was normally only twenty feet across and impossible to navigate in anything wider than a canoe. Now the biggest obstacles were tree branches and spiderwebs. We crouched behind the console and let them scrape and whip across the boat.

"We need to get an ambulance on the way, Dad."

He swatted a banana spider from his arm. "Yeah," he mumbled, thinking about something else.

"Curly told me they won't help out during the storm."

"The hell they won't."

"They can't get to the landing."

"I did," he said. "Take the wheel."

I took over driving while Dad ducked beneath the console and pulled out his handheld radio. "Curly," he said into it.

No one answered.

"Curly!" he shouted.

"Yeah?" came Curly's voice. "That you, Tom?"

"Yeah, it's me. I'm in trouble. Where can you get an ambulance down to the river? I'm bringing in the Stovall girls."

"What's goin' on?"

"One's snakebit and the other . . ." He looked at me.

"Hypothermia, I think. Lots of ant bites," I said.

"Hypothermic and ant bites."

"You on the river, Tom?"

"Listen, I don't have time to explain all this. Get me an ambulance. As close to the landin' as they can get."

"You know—"

"Don't give me that crap, Curly! Make it happen. You drive it yourself if you have to."

There was a pause. "All right, Tom. Let me see what I can do. Stand by."

Dad shoved the radio back under the console and took the steering wheel from me. He bumped more speed out of the throttle and we plowed ahead. He took a hard turn and I fell against the gunnel, wincing as the wound on my thigh pressed against the steel.

"Stay down on the deck," he said.

I got to my feet again. "I'm okay," I said.

"What happened to your leg?"

"That hog tusked me."

"We got to get somethin' on it."

I steadied myself and didn't answer him.

"Look under the console," he said. "There's a couple of towels. You need to warm up. They're wet, but they're better than nothin'."

"Later," I said.

The boat smashed and cracked through another mass of limbs. I pulled a net of sticky spiderwebs from my face, then looked back at the creek, trying to get some clue as to where we were by the pattern of the turns. I had a faint idea, but I knew we still had maybe a mile more to bull our way through.

The boat suddenly hit a log and threw us against the console.

"Aw, come on!" Dad said.

I started for the stern. He cut the throttle and toggled the electric lift on the outboard to raise the propeller out of the water while I got out of the boat and stood on a submerged log and shoved us over. As soon as I climbed aboard over the transom he lowered the motor and started ahead again.

"I don't know how we can get to them," I said. "It's like nothing you ever saw."

"I never gave it a thought," he said. "Where they'd all go."

"You're about to find out."

"Deer, too?"

"Yeah. And bears. There was a bear in the tree next to us."

Dad bit his lip again and shook his head.

"If the snakes haven't killed it. I think it's snakebit, too."

"Damn snakes," he said.

"They're all over the mound. I've never seen so many in one place."

Dad set his jaw again. "Sounds like we're about to go to war," he muttered.

"Yeah," I said. "Except we don't have any guns."

38

WHEN WE BROKE FROM THE TREES INTO BOTTLE
Creek the wind and rain came against our faces again,
but not so hard this time. I looked at the sky, and the gray
clouds seemed higher and less dense. Then I looked down
and refocused on where we were going.

"You think the trail's wide enough?" I said.

Dad gunned the boat downstream. "It'll have to be."

In a moment we arrived at the bend in the creek where
the trail started. I studied the trees, trying to find a break
in the canopy.

"Can you tell where it is?" Dad said.

I kept running my eyes over it all, using my imagination to redraw where the sandy footpath would be if it
weren't flooded over. Finally I thought I recognized the
crooked cypress that marked the trail.

I pointed. "The cypress tree. There."

Dad studied it. "Yeah," he said. "I think you got it."

He swung the boat toward the bank and plowed into
the foliage, and the swamp canopy closed over us again

like a protective cloak. The wind and rain grew quiet and distant. I began to listen. Gradually, I felt myself being pulled back into the nightmare.

"I hear it up there," Dad said.

Now squirrel and bird chatter filled the treetops. I looked up and saw the canopy was no longer being tossed and whipped about by the wind gusts. The smaller creatures were coming out. A hog squeal pierced the wetland, but I knew it wasn't Rusty. It was one of the smaller ones. Still alive.

Dad drifted off in thought, focusing on the tangle of wet green ahead, working the boat slowly through the trees.

"Go to the stern and break off the navigation light pole," he said. "Then snap the bulb off the top. Maybe I can sharpen the metal."

A cottonmouth plunked onto the bow and quickly slithered over the gunnels into the water.

Dad ducked reflexively. "Crap," he muttered.

He looked about in the trees. They were filled with small animals staring back at us. More snakes.

"Go ahead," he said. "Watch out for those things."

I went to the rear of the boat and broke off the light pole. I studied it doubtfully, but it was all we had. I broke off the bulb and was left with a three-foot length of aluminum pole the diameter of my thumb.

"I don't know how we're gonna sharpen it," I said.

"Just give it to me, then."

I passed the pole to him and went back up to the bow and studied the trees ahead.

"Liza!" I shouted. I didn't expect her to answer me. "I've got Dad! We're coming!"

Something crashed and squealed and grunted not fifty yards ahead. Two alligators glided away silently over the concentric rings of disturbance lapping against the boat.

"Look at the water," Dad said.

I glanced down and saw the bloody soup.

"I've seen it," I said.

"How'd you get out of here?"

I didn't answer him. Through the tangle of vines and tree branches I saw the dark shape of the mound.

Where's Rusty? I thought. *Where is he?*

39

"I SEE THE MOUND," I SAID.

"Liza!" he shouted. "Francie!"

There was no answer. Another squeal erupted from the mound. It seemed the level of noise and confusion was even more than when I'd left it that morning, especially with the squirrels fussing and birds flapping in the trees. It was all the chaos of a washed-out zoo.

"You can't get past that hog, Dad. He's up there. Don't ground the boat yet."

"What?"

"Back off!"

Dad slammed the boat into reverse just as it was about to nose into the base of the mound. In that instant a blur of rust-colored hair came charging down the hill, crashing through the underbrush. Rusty plowed into the water and slammed against the hull. I lost my footing and toppled into the water, falling across the back of the crazed hog. I sank and swirled in the murky depths, watching the white belly of the beast and its hooves slicing above me. I flipped and swam under the shadow of the boat and came up on the other side. I grabbed the gunnels and felt Dad's hand grip my arm and haul me into the boat once again.

"You hurt, son?"

I got to my knees and shook my head while I caught my breath.

"God almighty!" he said.

I looked across the bow to see Rusty wading ashore. The hog turned his black eyes to us, and I saw the crazed hate and rage twitching in his muscles. His face and tusks were red with blood.

"I've never seen anything snakebit act like that," Dad said.

I stood. "We've got to get the girls."

Dad dropped the pole on the deck. "This won't do us any good against that thing."

"Liza!" I called.

There was no answer. Dad walked to the bow of the boat and stared back at Rusty. The hog wheezed and grunted and pawed the mud.

"I got an idea," Dad said. He bent and picked up the bow rope and began making a loop on the end. "Get me closer."

"What are you doing?"

"I'm gonna get a noose around his head."

"You think you can hold it?"

"You got a better idea?"

I shook my head. I didn't. And I was desperate to try anything.

"I'm gonna drag him up to the boat and tie him off to this bow cleat."

I looked at Rusty again, staring as if he dared us to try anything. Dad straightened with the lasso formed in his hands.

"Go on," he said. "Get me closer."

"He's gonna come into the boat."

"Don't get me *that* close."

I bumped the boat into gear and pulled it back again. Just enough to give us a small thrust toward the mound. I kept my hand on the throttle, ready to reverse. Rusty wheezed and took a challenging step toward us.

"You just stay where you are, big nasty," Dad muttered.

The boat drifted closer until there was only fifteen feet between us and the hog.

"Bump it again," Dad said quietly.

I gave the engine another nudge and felt my heart beating in my chest.

"Get ready to reverse," he said.

When we were about ten feet from the hog Dad tossed the loop at him. The rope hit Rusty in the face, and he

175

snorted and wheeled to the right, leaving the line slack on the ground.

"Reverse!" Dad said.

But I was already backing off.

"This isn't gonna work!" I said, frustrated.

Dad gathered the rope again and studied Rusty as he re-formed the lasso.

"Get me in there again," he said. "Closer this time."

I sighed with hopelessness but started us forward again.

"Stand still, big boy," Dad said.

This time Dad didn't throw right away. We came within six feet of the hog and I saw the beast's muscles tensing. He wanted nothing more than to get into the boat with us. To tear us to pieces.

"Dad!"

He tossed the loop just as Rusty charged. The hog slammed into the bow and slipped and fell away. But the loop had gone around his head and one foreleg. Dad fell back and pulled on the rope with everything he had.

"Reverse!" he yelled.

I slammed the boat into reverse as Rusty squealed and swung his head and battered the side of the boat like someone beating a metal barrel with butcher knives. The hog had his feet on the ground and he was pulling against us. The boat swung around and the propeller locked on a tree limb and the engine went dead.

"Get us out of here!" Dad yelled.

I fumbled with the key and started the engine, but as soon as I put it in gear, it shut off again.

"It's hung!" I shouted.

I saw Dad's arms bucking and knocking against the struggle, his biceps bulging from the strain.

"Crap!" he cursed.

"Tie it!" I said.

Dad managed to sit up and rolled to the bow cleat and began wrapping the line.

"Go!" he yelled. "Go get the girls!"

40

I LEAPED OUT OF THE BOAT AND CLAWED MY WAY up the mound while behind me Rusty hammered against the boat in a fit of rage.

"Hurry!" Dad shouted. "I don't know how long this'll hold."

I passed one of the smaller hogs, lying in the palmetto, gored in the stomach and barely breathing.

"Liza!" I yelled.

I dreaded what I was about to see. I tried to shut out the gruesome images from my mind as I slipped and crawled steadily upward, not even looking for snakes.

When I reached the juniper my eyes went up into the branches. I saw the girls, hanging limply against the jacket straps.

"Liza!"

The girls weren't moving. Then I saw Liza open her eyes.

I felt my heart cave in my chest. I felt like crying, but I coughed and swallowed the feeling away.

"Hang on," I said. "Just hang on."

Even though Dad was still below, straining against Rusty, it seemed like it was all over. Like nothing else could go wrong. I climbed into the tree, and my feet found familiar footing on the crude platform where I'd spent the worst part of the worst night of my life.

"Hang on," I said again.

I balanced before them and fumbled with the strap buckles around Francie. She began to weep and whimper while my shaking fingers worked as fast as they could.

"We're getting out of here, Francie," I said.

I got her loose and put her under my arm and carried her to the ground. I placed her against the base of the juniper.

"I'll be back," I said.

Francie fell over and curled up in the leaves and pulled her knees up to her chest.

"Come on, Cort!" Dad yelled from below.

I stood and looked downhill. "I've got them! They're okay!"

"Hurry!"

I pulled myself into the tree again and began untying Liza. She gave me a weak smile.

"I knew you'd make it," she said.

"Don't talk," I said.

The strap came undone and she fell toward me. Perched precariously on the tree branch, I wasn't prepared for this. I clutched her against me with one arm and locked my fingers onto a limb overhead with every bit of strength I had. Slowly, my grip was overcome by her limp weight, and my fingers slipped. Both of us fell backward and crashed through limbs the full ten feet to the ground. I hit on my back with Liza landing heavily on top of me. I felt the wind knocked out of me and I lay there and stared dizzily at the treetops.

But it was nothing. After all we'd been through, it was nothing. Even though I was struggling to get my breath back, I felt like smiling.

Then I heard a metallic snap from below followed by a hollow pounding against the boat. Rusty squealed horrifically. I rolled away from Liza and lay on my stomach, trying to regain my senses through a fog of confusion.

"Cort!" Dad yelled. "Get off the ground!"

By the strain in his voice I knew Rusty was loose. In that same instant I heard the beast smashing through the underbrush, charging uphill.

I pushed myself up and grabbed the girls. I barely had time to shove them against the juniper before Francie screamed. I felt fear race electric up my spine and expected the hog to pitchfork me in the back at any moment. When I spun around I saw his bloody, torn face inches from my own.

41

I BREATHED IN THE STENCH OF RUSTY, DRIED blood and fetid river mud and sickness. As if making a final display of rage before taking our lives, he plunged his snout into the leaves and tore at the dirt with his tusks. I pressed back against the girls, shoving them closer to the trunk of the tree. In the distance I thought I heard Dad fighting his way uphill. This time my mind didn't search for options. It was locked with terror. I thought of nothing but the hog face.

"Cort!" Dad yelled from below.

Francie whimpered softly from behind my back. Rusty continued to squeal and grunt and rake his yellow tusks through the dirt. Images of the night before began to flip through my head like stills from a movie. Like it was time to put it all together one last time and try to make sense of it all. I remembered the houseboat, bobbing down the storm-thrashed river. The crash and the slog through the vast swamp. The terrifying sound and vision of the mound when we first came upon it. The look on Liza's face after I knocked the cottonmouth off her heel. Death constantly around us, coming for us . . . *There was no sense in it.*

A black blur appeared from nowhere and bowled into the hog. At first I didn't know what was happening. Then I couldn't believe what I was seeing.

"Elmo," I heard Francie say.

Bear and hog rolled in a tangled blur of snarling and squealing frenzy. Teeth and claws and tusks and hooves gleamed and slashed beside us like a whirlwind of knives. The fight was so fast and violent and unpredictable that I was too shocked to move.

"Cort!" Dad yelled again.

I looked downhill, but I couldn't see him. Then Elmo came rolling in front of us and in an instant the hog was on top of him, burying and slashing with his cutter teeth on the bear's chest. I turned to Liza and Francie. I realized immediately there was no way I could get them back into the juniper. I shoved them sideways.

"Around the tree!" I said.

Francie began to crawl while Liza stared at me, dazed and disoriented. I stood and grabbed her and dragged her after Francie. We didn't get far before the bear got to his feet and spun and bowled the hog over again. This time the two beasts came so close I felt one of them hit my leg. I waited for the pain to come. Then I drew the courage to look at my shin and saw that it was unwounded.

"Stay still!" Dad yelled.

I looked to my left and saw him standing not ten yards away, holding a useless stick. His face was stricken with horror. I sat against the girls and turned my eyes back to the battle. The bear was on top now, clamping the hog's throat with his teeth and swatting at him with his claws. The hog bucked and squirmed and squealed, its feet kicking clumps of muddy leaves over our laps.

"Cort!"

I glanced at Dad again. There was nothing he could do. We were pinned between the tree and the two beasts fighting to the death.

The hog managed to get on top again and I thought I detected the bear weakening. The wounds in his chest were deep, and his fur was wet and matted and gleaming a purplish color from all the blood. While the hog had gaping wounds about his body from the tearing claws, he didn't seem slowed. I was certain he'd outlast our big friend.

The bear grabbed the hog by the throat and there was something different about his hold this time. Rusty's body tensed like an electric shock had passed through him.

The hog's legs straightened and twitched. The squealing stopped, and all I heard was the growling of the bear through clenched teeth and a strained gurgling sound from the hog. The bear sensed he had crushed something vital. He rolled on top again, shook his head, clamped down, and snarled viciously. Rusty's crazed eyes grew wide and white as quail eggs, flooded with a suffocating look of desperation.

My optimism flared. "Come on, Elmo," I said anxiously.

It suddenly occurred to me how foolish it was to take sides. The bear was just as sick and crazed as Rusty. Our imagined friendship with the beast was something born out of desperation. He wasn't three feet from us, and there was no reason he wouldn't turn and do to us just what he was doing to the hog.

I saw Dad edging around the fight, trying to reach us. There was no way I could get both of the girls down the hill alone.

"I'm comin', Cort," he said.

The bear kept his lock on the hog, his snarls sounding more like weak sighs. Rusty gurgled and kicked occasionally, the life slowly leaving him.

"Francie," I whispered, "can you crawl over to me?"

She didn't answer and I turned and looked at her.

"Elmo saved us," she said.

"That's right," I said. "Now it's time to go home."

I reached out for her and pulled her into my lap. At the same time Dad was rushing around the back side of the juniper. He grabbed Liza and pulled her to him.

"Get up, Cort," he said. "Go."

I studied the bear again. I saw his eyes watching me, as if wondering what I was waiting for.

"I got Francie," I said.

Dad hurried away through the underbrush with Liza over his shoulder. I slowly stood with Francie and side-stepped from out between Elmo and the tree. The bear continued to clamp the hog's throat even though Rusty was clearly dead.

"Is Elmo going to die?" Francie said.

"Shhh," I said.

I backed across the clearing of torn dirt and bloody leaves, watching the bear. As if he sensed I was safely away, he released his hold and laid his chin across our dead enemy. His big chest heaved and his breathing came out rough and bubbly. His eyes closed and opened and looked at us.

"We need to help him, Cort," Francie said.

The thought had crossed my mind. Even though I knew the bear was going to die, it seemed the right thing to do. But it wasn't. It was foolish to think I had any control over the natural way of life and death out here in the swamp. Like Dad had told me, we'd pulled back the curtain and I'd found what he had warned me about. I'd seen it now. And it was time to close the curtain again and leave it as it was. And never take it for granted again.

I turned away and shifted Francie higher.

"He's going to be okay," I told her.

She rested her chin on my shoulder and I stepped down-hill into the palmetto.

42

CURLY RADIOED THAT TWO AMBULANCES WERE waiting for us at a bridge three miles south of the landing. Here the highway crossed a wide drainage basin far enough off the river that we'd avoid working against the turbulent current of the Tensaw. We had the girls on the floor of the jon with a towel around them. Liza's leg was gruesomely swollen and she was slipping in and out of consciousness.

When we arrived at the bridge we found the floodwater almost over the highway. The ambulance lights strobed red and white through the drizzling rain like they were floating in the middle of it. We pulled up against the roadway level with the medics, and they stepped over the guardrail and loaded the girls onto two stretchers. One of the medics asked me what type of snake it was. I told them, and they gave Liza a shot of something.

"Go with 'em," Dad told me. "Get your leg taken care of."

I didn't answer him. Suddenly I couldn't make sense of

anything. I couldn't believe there was nothing left for me to do. But my mind already realized it, and I collapsed in the boat. Everything went black.

I kept my eyes closed for what seemed like hours, listening to the steady beeping of hospital equipment. When I opened them I found myself alone within a partition, facing a curtain. I heard people talking softly around me. I saw feet pass the base of the curtain. I closed my eyes again.

Some time later I felt a hand on my shoulder. I saw Dad standing over me.

"Hey, bud," he said.

"Hey."

"How you feelin'?"

I cocked my eyes about the room and didn't answer him.

"You've been out for nearly twenty-four hours. It's Wednesday mornin'."

My head was groggy and it took a moment to make sense of where I was and how I'd gotten there. Then the memory of everything that happened flooded over me.

I looked at him. "Are they okay?"

"They're fine," he said.

"What about Liza's leg?"

"She's gonna be fine."

"Will she lose it?"

"They don't think so."

I struggled to recall everything I should be concerned about.

The girls were safe. Dad was standing over me.

I slowly realized it was really over. It was all over. For the first time in a week I felt free in my head.

"They've still got some heat blankets on you," Dad said. "Doc told me all of you are lucky you didn't die from hypothermia."

I smirked. Dad knew what I was thinking.

"Well, they stitched up the gash on your leg and the cut on your hand. You should be good as new in no time."

The curtain parted and Mrs. Stovall walked in. She moved to the other side of my bed and put her hand on my cheek.

"Thank you, Cort," she said.

I was glad they were with me, but I didn't want to talk to them or anybody else. I just wanted to lie there and not think about it all. And sleep again.

43

JUST AFTER NOON ON WEDNESDAY DAD BROUGHT me a change of clothes and set them next to my bed.

"You about ready?" he asked. "The doctor says you're good to go."

"Yeah," I said. "I'm ready."

Shortly after that a nurse arrived and detached the IV from my arm and made notes on a chart. After she left, Dad helped me up and I got dressed.

"Will they let me see Liza?"

"Prob'ly not a good time," he said. "We better stay out of their way."

The day after a hurricane is always strange for me. The sky is deep blue and the air is crisp and dry. It seems the storm sucked away everything, leaving a bluebird day to proudly showcase the destruction left in its wake.

Dad drove us slowly up the highway, stopping for

utility trucks and easing past piles of storm debris stacked along the ditch. We had to take a back road and wind around to the north end of the county and come south again.

"I've been wondering," I said. "How'd you know we were in trouble?"

"I had a feeling somethin' was wrong," he said. "I just knew it. I left the truck here and walked in. I saw the garage door open and the generator run out. Nobody inside the house. Then I found the boat trailer smashed up at the bottom of the ramp and the houseboat gone."

"Francie got her wrist caught in Catfish's leash. He drug her out into the storm, and she got onto the houseboat before it broke loose . . . That started it all. We got on the river and caught up with it, but everything got worse after that."

"Glad you got off."

I looked at him. "I hated you, Dad. I hated you for leaving me like that."

He put his hand on my shoulder and I felt myself starting to tear up at the memory of it all.

"It won't happen again," he said. "You're the most important thing in the world to me."

I sniffled and wiped my nose with the back of my hand.

"You got every right to be mad."

I nodded. "I'm okay now," I said. "Let's not talk about it anymore."

Dad pulled his hand away and nodded considerately.

After nearly an hour Dad got us back to Nelson Morton's cow pasture, where he parked near the fence.

"Think you can walk to the house with those stitches?"

"I can make it," I said.

We left the truck and crossed the pasture. From there we walked an old logging road to the back side of the Stovalls' property. When we arrived at the landing I saw the river had receded somewhat. The bait shop and the boat slip docks were gone. Lumber and storm debris were tangled in the trees and scattered through the clearing. The launch ramp was coated with mud and trash. The sight of it was overwhelming.

"Looks bad," I said.

"We've got some work ahead of us, that's for sure."

"Let's rest a minute."

"Go ahead and sit down," he said. "No rush."

We sat at the top of the hill.

"Linda told me we could stay at her place until we get things figured out," Dad said.

"We have insurance or anything like that?"

"Well, not exactly anything like that."

"What are you gonna do?"

"Paul Davis has an RV he said we could use for a while. I can bring that over tomorrow once we get the road cleared."

"All right," I said. "Then what?"

"What you think about buildin' a house?"

"A house? Where?"

"Around here somewhere. Linda said she'd sell us a half acre or so."

"How you gonna pay for that?"

"I don't have to do it all at once."

"How you gonna pay for a house?"

"There's gonna be plenty of cleanup work for a few months. A man with a chain saw can get after it and do pretty good. Good enough to get started, anyway."

I stared out over the dirty river.

"You're not doing it for Mom, are you?"

Dad picked up a twig and snapped it and let the pieces fall between his legs.

"I prob'ly should have done it a long time ago," he said.

"I don't think it would have helped."

He grinned. "Prob'ly not," he said.

The more I thought about it, Dad's idea about the house didn't sound too far-fetched. We'd built camp houses before. We knew how to frame and wire and plumb.

"We can do it, Dad."

He put his arm around me. "Man," he said, "a couple of nights ago when I was up the road at your mother's house, I was sittin' there watchin' the storm, worryin' about you kids. And it was just all empty there, you know. I mean, your mother was there, and Linda, but it was just empty."

I drew my knees up and studied the tips of my shoes.

"Your mom and I used to be happy together," Dad continued. "Believe it or not. But we just won't ever be that way again. I think I've finally got my head around that. Sometimes things just don't work out no matter how much you want 'em to."

"Yeah," I said.

"You gonna be any good around here with a bum leg and one hand?"

"I'll be fine," I said. "Let's get this place cleaned up."

44

DAD GOT MR. STOVALL'S OLD CHAIN SAW WORKING and spent until late afternoon clearing the road into the landing. I had a slight limp, and my leg was sore, but I was able to help. I put a glove on my hand with the stitches and could pick up some of the lighter trash. We used the Stovalls' truck until we were able to drive ours down. Then we got both of them working, hauling debris from the yard and tossing it in a burn pile near the river. Much of the lumber we found was still good, and we made a separate stack of boards to clean of nails and salvage. We'd use them to help rebuild the bait shop and the dock.

It was going to be days before the utility lines were restored. Just before dark I refueled the generator while Dad wired it directly into the house's electrical box. When he was done I started it, and we had power throughout the entire house.

Once we cleaned up and got settled Dad called the hospital to check on the girls. Mrs. Stovall told him she'd be bringing Francie home in the morning. They were going to keep Liza for a few more days.

After Dad hung up the phone he went over to the sofa and fell onto it heavily.

"I'm beat, son," he said.

"We can get the boards off the windows in the morning," I said. "Where we sleeping tonight?"

"I'm sleepin' right here."

"I'll take the floor, then. You hungry?"

"Maybe."

"I've got a few cans of soup I brought up from the houseboat. I'll get 'em out of the garage."

I walked through the pantry and opened the garage door. Catfish strolled past me, his toenails clicking across the linoleum like he'd only been gone a few minutes. He was wet and muddy, and briars were tangled and matted into his hair.

"Catfish!" I shouted.

He stopped and turned. I knelt and he came to me and I hugged him to my chest. I saw Dad's feet approach.

"I'll be damned," he said.

I rubbed my dog's neck, and he whined and cowered into me like he suddenly remembered all he'd been through.

"Looks like he's wore out," Dad said.

"Come on, boy," I said. "Let's get you cleaned up and get you something to eat."

I gave Catfish a bath outside the garage, rubbing him down and feeling for any major injuries. Aside from some welts on his body and scratches on his face, he seemed okay.

"You're sleeping with me tonight," I told him as I got some food ready for him.

He trembled with excitement.

"Nobody's leaving anybody again."

Dad rose early the next morning to go get the RV. I was taking the plywood off the house windows when Mrs. Stovall's car pulled up. Francie got out carrying her Elmo doll. She had a few small bandages on her face and arms, but otherwise she looked healthy. I lowered my hammer and went to meet them.

"How you feeling, Francie?"

She looked around. "This place looks terrible, Cort. You need to clean this up," she bossed.

Mrs. Stovall and I both laughed.

"I didn't know you'd be home so soon," I said. "I tried to get it ready for you."

"Where's Catfish?" Francie asked matter-of-factly.

I looked at Mrs. Stovall. "You told her?"

She shrugged her shoulders and widened her eyes with a look that said, *Not me.*

"He's around here somewhere," I said to Francie. "He's been looking for you."

"I know," she said flatly.

Mrs. Stovall approached me and rolled her eyes. "I think she's feelin' just fine, Cort. A little full of herself after all the attention she got at the hospital."

"Good," I said. "How about Liza?"

"She's better. I'll go sit with her tonight. They think I can bring her home on Sunday."

"Maybe we'll be off generator power by then. Just let me know if you need me to crank it. Dad should be back with an RV soon."

"Okay," she said. "You two feel free to use the house for anything you need."

"You go by Mom's place?"

"No, but she was fine when I left."

"Dad knows she's not coming back."

Mrs. Stovall nodded.

"She's prob'ly happier now. I guess I ought to go by there in a couple of days. See if she needs any help."

"That would be nice," she said.

I looked at my shoes. "Think she'll move on eventually?"

"I don't know, Cort. But sometimes people get along better than ever with a little distance."

"I'm not counting on it."

"This isn't the life for everybody," she added.

"I know. But Dad says it's in our blood."

"Your dad can be a little extreme."

"Yes, ma'am. I know."

45

THE UTILITY COMPANY RESTORED POWER TO THE house that weekend. By Sunday morning Dad and I had the landing mostly clear of debris and the RV parked near where the bait shop used to be. The river was finally flowing at a normal level, but it was muddy and foamy and thick like chocolate milk. The yammering of chain saws and the beeping of utility trucks rode the crisp fall air, and I knew those sounds would carry into the winter and through the spring.

Liza came home Sunday afternoon. Her entire left leg was bandaged and braced. I knew the doctors had cut it and pinned it open to relieve the swelling. Then they'd sewn it back together. She'd keep the leg, but she'd always have a scar from her foot to her thigh.

I helped her off the backseat while Mrs. Stovall held her crutches and Dad went to open the front door of the house. Francie stood behind us, watching.

"Hey," Liza said to me.

It was awkward seeing her. There was a lot I wanted to say, but I didn't know how or where to start.

"How you feeling?" I said.

She gave me a weak smile. "Okay."

"Catfish is home," Francie said.

I got under Liza's arm and helped her stand. I heard her gasp and hesitated.

"You okay?"

"Yes," she said after a moment. "I'm okay."

"Cort said Catfish didn't get back until Wednesday," Francie said.

"Go inside, Francie," Mrs. Stovall said. "Get the pillows off Liza's bed and put them on the sofa."

Mrs. Stovall passed Liza the crutches and she steadied herself on them. Then we all helped her inside. Once she was settled onto the living room sofa, Dad and I left Mrs. Stovall to finish getting her comfortable. We walked down to the riverbank without speaking. I followed him to a stack of salvaged lumber that we'd been de-nailing. It was hard to get the gruesome thought of Liza's leg operation out of my head. I could tell Dad was thinking about the same thing. He grabbed a hammer and shook his head. "She's lucky to still have it," he said.

I made hamburgers for us in the RV that evening. After

dinner I walked uphill again. I found Liza alone in the living room, lying on the sofa watching television.

"You need anything?" I asked her.

"I'd like to get up for a little bit," she said. "Let's go on the porch."

I helped her to the front door and onto the porch. We sat on the rough boards with our backs against the wall, looking over the landing and the river and swamp beyond.

"Dad's gonna build a house," I told her. "The RV's just temporary."

"Mom told me about it," she said.

"It might take a while."

Neither of us said anything for a moment.

"I don't want you to be scared of any of the stuff that happened," I said.

"I'm not scared," she said.

"Do you still wanna move?"

She looked at me. She shook her head.

"No?"

"No. Not if you're here."

"I'm here," I said. "I'm not going anywhere. But all that out there was just a bunch of bad luck. It could never happen like that again in a hundred years."

"I'm not scared of that," she said. "I mean, it's hard

not having a father around. It's scary in a different kind of way. Especially in a place like this."

"I know what you mean," I said.

"It's like riding in a car without your seat belt. I mean, you don't think you'll wreck, but you think about not having the seat belt on. You feel it."

"I think Dad's gonna be better for both of us now that Mom's gone."

"As long as you're here, I'm fine."

I looked at her. "Yeah?"

"You make me feel safe."

"I do?"

"Yeah. That's all I want."

"That's all?"

She nodded.

"What if I asked you to the fall party?"

She made that cute smile. "Ask me."

"Do you wanna go to the fall party?"

"Of course I do. Why didn't you ask me last year?"

"Well, I thought—"

"I had to go with Jason. All he did was talk to everybody but me the whole night."

Something freed in my chest like sprung rubber bands. I looked at the ground and chuckled to myself.

"Okay," I said.

Liza grabbed my hand and squeezed it. I felt warm all over.

"And you have to get your mom to take you to basketball practice, Cort. You're too good to quit."

"I didn't quit."

"You know what I mean."

"I don't think that's gonna happen," I said. "But I've already been thinking about it. And I've got a plan. It's kind of crazy, but it might work."

46

THAT NIGHT DAD SLEPT ON THE SOFA WHILE I LAY beneath him on the floor with Catfish beside me.

"Dad?" I said quietly.

"Yeah, son?"

"What do you think about what the bear did?"

"What do you mean?"

"Do you think he saved us?"

"Maybe," he finally said. "I've seen stranger things happen."

"It doesn't make sense."

"You havin' a hard time gettin' it out of your head?"

"There's a lot in my head. I thought about what you said . . . About pulling back the curtain. About how it can get evil real fast. I never knew what you meant before."

"Yeah, that swamp's not any place man was meant to survive for long."

"Maybe that's why the Indians left Bottle Creek."

"Maybe."

"Maybe it happened to them. The same thing."

"Somethin' sure run 'em off, didn't it?"

I could tell Dad was sleepy, but I had too much on my mind. I looked at the ceiling. "Do you ever think Mom was right? That maybe we should move?"

Dad rolled over and looked at me. " 'Cause of what happened in that hurricane?"

"No . . . Because maybe this isn't an easy place to live."

"What do *you* think?" he said.

"I think you'll always wanna be here."

"No. I mean, what do you think is the right thing to do?"

I turned back to him. "I love this place, Dad . . . But I wish I was around other kids more. If I could just get to basketball practice, or anything like that, it'd be enough."

"Uh-huh," Dad said.

"I've thought about driving the Stovalls' boat down-river and docking at Stimpson's. It'd only be about a mile to school from there. I'd have to watch the weather, but it'd be a way."

Dad studied me.

"I mean, it'd be weird, but it'd be a way for me to do it," I said.

"I'll take you," he said.

"But you've got to work."

"Look, your mother ain't comin' back. It don't appear

she's gonna be much help where she is either. Way I'm seein' it, we got one less mouth to feed. So I can spend a little less time on the river."

I looked at the ceiling again and smiled to myself.

"You good with that?" he said. And I heard the satisfaction in his tone.

"Yeah," I said. "I'm good with that."

"Hey, Cort?"

"Yes, sir?"

"I don't expect you to be a river guide like your old man. It ain't for everybody. You do what you wanna do."

"You're not old."

"You heard me."

"I know. Thanks, Dad."

As I lay there in the dark it occurred to me just how much a few blurry pieces can ruin a picture. Now, with everything coming into focus, my image of life at the landing went from something I wanted to get away from to something I was proud of again. My heart swelled for the days ahead. Basketball with the guys in the gym. The fall party with Liza. Dry October leaves drifting out of the trees into the river. Gusty breezes sending patches of ripples across the calm black water of the swamp.

Dad began to snore and I imagined that I was still on the houseboat, sleeping in the bunk above him. I missed the soothing sounds of the frogs and the crickets. I missed the water against the pontoons. And I started to imagine how we could build a new house so that we didn't completely lose touch with the river at night. Something out of wood, maybe. A house with a screen sleeping porch.

"Dad?" I whispered.

He continued to snore. I wanted to tell him how good I felt about it all. I wanted to tell him he was right, the delta was in my blood. It was my home, and there's something comforting about a place you've lived your entire life, as long as the people you love are with you. Take them away, and it's hard to figure out where you belong.

I didn't know if I wanted to be a river guide, and it didn't matter that I didn't know. I had plenty of time to figure it out. And everybody I needed was sleeping around me, and they'd be there for me no matter what I did. What I decided.

Author's Note

I've been through more hurricanes than I can remember. They come with life on the Gulf Coast. Even as I began to write this novel, Hurricane Karen was just off the tip of Louisiana, about to make landfall. As the storm approached, I wrote down some impressions.

The storm arrives tomorrow and will sweep over our house on Sunday. It is 8 a.m. and out my office window I see the sky is blue and cloudless. The storm is still hundreds of miles away, but there is already a sense that something is not right. The birds are quiet and the squirrels aren't twitching about in the yard. The air is too still and heavy. It seems that everything is already cowering before this unseen chaos rolling toward us. As the old saying goes, it is the calm before the storm. Late this afternoon bands of clouds will arrive. Intermittent rain will patter the leaves. I'll have boarded up most of the windows by then, but I

won't park the cars in the garage until tomorrow,
when the police force everyone off the roads.

I have a mental checklist of things I do before a hurricane. The routine has been the same for years: make sure you have enough plywood for windows before the lumber store runs out, fill the jerricans with gasoline, get the boats out of the water, and get everything off the dock.

Once the rain starts it won't stop for days. For those who stay, there's nothing to do but board up your windows and get inside your box and wait it out. Even though I've always lived on the coast, I have only evacuated once. I was eight years old when my father drove our family to the north end of Baldwin County in front of Hurricane Frederic. We stayed at a friend's house in the country. All night the rain pelted the windows and tree limbs fell on the roof. When we woke the next morning it looked like a bomb had gone off outside. Days passed before the roads were cleared and we were able to make our way south again. When we arrived at our home there was not a pine tree standing. I remember thinking it looked like a giant had crushed them beneath his feet like blades of grass. Where there used to be a lawn was now mud and sand. Pieces of people's houses and docks were wedged in the trees. It didn't seem possible to clean it all up.

We went ten days without power. Since the electric

pump on the well wouldn't work, Mom boiled water from the bay to use for washing. We had clean drinking water in the bathtub, which Dad had filled before we left. Our meals were limited to canned food and powdered milk. But I was just a kid and it was all an adventure to me.

Dad worked on clearing the trees while I shoveled mud out of the yard with my siblings. For months afterward the crisp winter air was filled with the sound of chain saws and trucks. It was heavy with the smell of briny bay water and diesel and two-cycle oil. And slowly, like a place swarmed with worker ants, the trash disappeared and our house stood in a leafless land of brown, not to be green again until spring.

While hurricanes are nothing new to any of us down here, there is an aspect of them that still fascinates me. North of us is the Mobile-Tensaw Delta, a two-hundred-fifty-thousand-acre swamp, second in size only to the Mississippi River Delta. It is filled with deer, wild hogs, alligators, snakes, bears, and countless other, smaller animals like squirrels, raccoons, opossums, and nutria. During hurricanes the storm surge from Mobile Bay backs as much as ten feet of water over it. Where do all the animals go?

My imagination has them swimming the perimeter rivers like caribou, climbing the high bluffs and standing about terrified on people's green lawns. But I've never seen or heard of this happening. For the most part, they stay out there. I know from seeing their bloated bodies in the river that many of them drown, but most don't. After the floodwater drains away, the swamp seems as healthy as ever. How did they survive?

I got my answer one day. It was late in the afternoon before a hurricane was supposed to hit. It was already gusting and drizzling rain. I was at the river landing where I keep my boat, waiting my turn to back my trailer down the landing ramp into the water. Everyone was in a hurry to get their equipment out and up to high ground.

There was one man waiting to put his boat in. He was a rough-looking character dressed in full camouflage, watching the rest of us like he didn't know anyone and didn't care to. In his boat was a sadistic-looking Catahoula dog and beside it was a single-shot twelve gauge shotgun.

"You about to go out in this stuff?" I asked him.

"Best huntin' day of the year," he said.

"For what?"

"Every danged thing in this swamp's headed to high ground. Like shootin' fish in a barrel."

But I couldn't think of any high ground for miles. As far as I knew it was flat marsh.

"Where do you go?" I asked him.

"Sand Hill," he said. "Alligator Ridge. There's places out there."

I was vaguely familiar with both of the spots he mentioned: grown-over mounds of dredge spoil from a channel cut during the Second World War. Most people hadn't heard of them; fewer knew how to find them.

Ever since that conversation I've been fascinated with what it must be like to see all of those swamp creatures, predators and prey, crowded together on a tip of high ground. As with any large, densely vegetated, unpopulated wilderness, there are rumors of other, more unlikely creatures. The black panther . . . coatimundi . . . Sasquatch.

Would they be there?

But *Terror at Bottle Creek* is not a story about strange creatures. I kept it realistic. It's an account of how I now imagine things are out in the Mobile-Tensaw Delta during a fictional hurricane. I've changed the names of a few locations, but otherwise they all exist. I did not change the name of the Bottle Creek Indian Mounds. You'll want to look those up for yourself.

Watt Key
Point Clear, Alabama